The ONLY THING WORSE Than Witches

LAUREN MAGAZINER

DIAL BOOKS
FOR YOUNG READERS
an imprint of Penguin Group (USA) LLC

DIAL BOOKS FOR YOUNG READERS
Published by the Penguin Group
Penguin Group (USA) LLC
375 Hudson Street
New York, New York 10014

USA / Canada / UK / Ireland / Australia / New Zealand / India / South Africa / China

penguin.com

A Penguin Random House Company

Library of Congress Cataloging-in-Publication Data

Magaziner, Lauren.
The only thing worse than witches / Lauren Magaziner.   pages cm
Summary: Eleven-year-old Rupert cannot resist applying to an advertisement
to be a witch's apprentice, but quickly finds himself over his head with the young
witch-in-training who desperately needs his help.
ISBN 978-0-8037-3918-5 (hardcover)
[1. Witchcraft—Fiction. 2. Apprentices—Fiction. 3. Magic–Fiction. 4. Best
friends—Fiction. 5. Friendship—Fiction. 6. Mothers and sons—Fiction.] I. Title
PZ7.M2713Onl 2014   [Fic]—dc23   2013034310

Printed in the United States of America
1 3 5 7 9 10 8 6 4 2

Designed by Mina Chung • Text set in Perpetua Std

To Mom, Dad, and Michael,
for many magical years of endless inspiration,
laughter, and—most importantly—love

The
ONLY
THING
WORSE
Than
Witches

The Worst
Assignment Ever

RUPERT WAS DOWN IN THE DUMPS. LITERALLY.

The garbage from Gliverstoll's town dump sloshed around his ankles, and piles and piles of trash extended as far as he could see. Rupert reached forward to peel something slimy off a bicycle handle, all the while lamenting his horrible luck. Why did he have to be in Class B with the dreadful Mrs. Frabbleknacker? Everyone in Class A had Miss Snugglybuns—and she was supposedly the nicest, most wonderful teacher who ever lived. Rupert heard that Miss Snugglybuns baked her students a four-layer cake every single day. And during science class, she brought in a big lamp and a watering can to help her class make rainbows.

But no. Rupert was stuck with Mrs. Frabbleknacker, who thought that the best way to teach waste management was to make her science class find a paper clip buried somewhere in the town dump.

Rupert grumbled under his breath as he sunk his hands into a brown pile that looked suspiciously like poo. *Mrs. Frabbleknacker*, he thought, *is the worst person I have ever met*. It wasn't the first time Rupert thought this, and he was sure it wouldn't be the last. He hated her with every cell in his body, with every bacteria now crawling on his skin. Because Mrs. Frabbleknacker was:

1. Extremely mean. Once when Allison Gormley passed a note to Kaleigh Brown, Mrs. Frabbleknacker made them both stand on their heads for the entire class period. When they finally turned right side up, their faces were purple and their words came out backward. ("I LEEF LUFWA!" said Allison. "EM OOT!" said Kaleigh.) It took them a whole week to learn how to speak normally again.

2. Extremely scary. She was the scariest-looking adult that Rupert had ever seen. She was tall, thin,

and hunched, like a coat rack that didn't know how to stand up straight. Mrs. Frabbleknacker had a very knobbly, criggly nose that twisted off in a thousand different directions. She also had a long, spindly tongue that she liked to stick out at the children in her class. Her hair was dark and straight and as rigid as cardboard. She had pale skin as wrinkly as tinfoil and as clammy as spit. Whenever she clomped past Rupert's desk, he caught the faint scent of belly-button lint, and her breath always smelled like mushy bananas.

3. Extremely strange. While the other fifth-grade class got to keep frogs as pets, Mrs. Frabbleknacker made her class dissect their frogs. Rupert's class had to carefully pull out the organs and put them into buckets for each different frog part. Rupert's hand had trembled as he pulled the tiny frog heart away from the tiny frog lung. And he tried desperately not to poke through the tiny frog stomach. When the day was done, Mrs. Frabbleknacker had collected twenty-six hearts, intestines, stomachs, livers, and tongues. She had twice as many eyes and lungs, and four times as many legs—all in their respective buckets. Rupert saw her loading the buckets of frog

parts into her trunk after school, and he couldn't help but imagine a framed collection of frog guts hanging on Mrs. Frabbleknacker's walls.

4. Extremely dangerous. Mrs. Frabbleknacker had a temper like a hurricane, especially when it came to the witches. She always talked about how angry the witches made her, and how much she loathed certain ones. And once, when Hal Porter mentioned the Fairfoul Witch in her class, Mrs. Frabbleknacker turned red, picked Hal up by the scruff of his shirt, and tossed him out of the classroom.

Rupert hated her all the time, but he hated her most of all at this very moment as he dug his hands through sludge to find a stupid paper clip.

"This gives a whole new meaning to needle in a haystack, doesn't it?" said poor, brave Bruno Gopp as he walked over to where Rupert and Kaleigh were silently digging through trash. Bruno was a boy in Rupert's class, and Rupert thought that he was almost too brave for his own good—he actually *volunteered* to answer questions Mrs. Frabbleknacker asked.

"Shhhh!" Kaleigh snapped. "You don't want her to catch us talking. You saw what she did to me and Allison."

"Aw, I'm not scared of her."

"You should be," Kaleigh whispered. "Did you hear what happened to her husband?"

"Who's crazy enough to marry her?" Bruno said, a bit too loudly.

Kaleigh clamped a hand over his mouth. "Shhhh!"

"What happened to her husband?" Rupert asked.

Kaleigh dropped her voice so low that Rupert could hardly hear her. "No one knows."

"Maybe she killed him," Bruno said.

"Maybe she keeps him locked in the basement and feeds him through a hole in the wall," Rupert suggested.

"I don't think she's really married," Kaleigh whispered. "She's probably just faking it." Bruno snorted, and Kaleigh hushed him again. "Shush, Bruno!"

"Kaleigh's right. We shouldn't talk," Rupert said. "We need to focus on finding the paper clip, already. At least whoever finds the paper clip gets to go home—"

"But what about the rest of us?" Bruno asked. "Do we have to stay here all night?"

"Maybe," Rupert said. "But I'd rather someone go home than no one."

Bruno thought about this for a moment and sighed. "When I get home, I'm going to eat a hot dog."

"I'm going to take a bath," Kaleigh volunteered.

"I'm going to lock myself in my room and demand to be homeschooled," Rupert said.

"And *I'm* going to drop-kick three naughty children so hard, you'll land on the witches' doorstep, and I'll let them tear you to pieces," Mrs. Frabbleknacker snarled from behind them.

Rupert closed his eyes, wishing that Mrs. Frabbleknacker actually *would* kick him to the witches' doorstep. Anything would be better than this.

Gliverstoll

HOURS LATER, RUPERT WALKED HOME FROM THE
dump, dripping a trail of brown sludge in his wake.
Still, even though he was sopping wet and disturb-
ingly slimy, his spirits cheered as he walked through
his town.

Rupert had always loved Gliverstoll. His town was
built into a rocky mountain nestled by the ocean.
Most of the hustle and bustle of Gliverstoll took place
in the shops around Main Beach. Rupert's house,
though, was at the tippy-top of the mountain, quite
far away from the beach. The dump was close to the
bottom, so Rupert had a long way home, zigzagging
up the roads that wound around the mountain.

Rupert could tell from the dusky sun that it was already pretty late. He figured that his mother would be at home by now, but he quickly peeked inside the quilt shop—where she worked—anyway.

Mrs. Marmalin, his mom's boss, was sweeping up the shop with a broom. Rupert tried the door, but it was locked—so he ended up knocking until she noticed he was outside.

"Rupert!" she said when she opened the door. She gracefully wiped her hands on her quilted apron and adjusted her wire-rimmed glasses as she looked at him. "What are you doing out so late? And by your-self, too!"

"I'm coming from the dump," Rupert said. "My teacher made us dig for a paper clip."

Mrs. Marmalin laughed. "Of course, dear. Of course," she said, as though Rupert was making the whole thing up.

Rupert looked around the dimly lit store. "Is my mom here?"

"She went home hours ago, poor thing. Spooked by a witch!"

"A witch?" Rupert said.

"One of the witches walked into our shop today

and demanded that we sell her one of our finest quilts at a price much less than it was worth. When I refused, of course, she went on a rampage. A terribly nasty temper."

"My mom left after that?"

"Oh, yes, she was terribly skittish. She said that she needed to lie down, and she looked so pale that I couldn't refuse. I wish I could have closed up shop and taken a breather myself, but these quilts don't sell themselves."

Rupert nodded.

"Thank you! Have a good night!" he said politely, and he backed out of her store.

Rupert walked to the end of Druscle Close and started up one of the curvy roads that led up the mountain. All the while, he thought about his mother running home from the quilting shop. He was surprised that she went home early—out of her three jobs, her sales work at the quilting store was his mother's absolute favorite. His mother loved to quilt, and she quilted all of the bedspreads and drapes in their house. It was her dream to make the longest quilt in the world.

Her second job was as an ice-cream taster at the

local ice-cream store. The makers of the ice cream could not test their own flavors because, ironically, Mr. and Mrs. Gummyum both had diabetes from eating too much of their own ice cream. So his mother got to taste all of their innovative flavors, like Nutty Butter Gumdrop, Sugar Salt, and Bologna Macaroni (which was their most popular flavor).

Her third job was a fortune-cookie writer. Her work for that had to be so secret that she signed fifteen contracts, swearing confidentiality. Rupert wasn't allowed to tell anyone either. In fact, he wasn't even supposed to know. It was like working as a spy—whenever his mother turned up for work, she had to go through five full-body scans, just to make sure that she didn't bring any microphones, telephones, cameras, or recording devices with her.

Despite all the secrecy, his mother enjoyed writing fortunes and often came home with stacks of fortune cookies that she brought to show Rupert. On those days, Rupert and his mother would crack mountain loads of fortune cookies in the kitchen.

Generally, Rupert's favorite fortunes were the ones that were very cryptic. His mom wrote one once that said *The mug is under the sofa.* Rupert loved that one. Sometimes he repeated it over and over again in his head. He had asked his mother where she got the inspiration to write something so fascinating, but she had said that that fortune was just a mistake. She was trying to direct her supervisors as to where she put her coffee cup, and the voice-recording program mistook that as a fortune. The machine had already printed two hundred copies before his mother realized what had gone wrong. Rupert was very disappointed to hear that, but he didn't tell her because she was most proud of her non-accidental fortunes.

He cringed as he thought about some of his mother's most prized work:

Tomorrow is a bright sunshiny day. Embrace it with bright sunshiny smiles.

(Rupert thought that one was a little cheesy.)

You are very loved.

(Rupert thought that one was even cheesier.)

You are unique and beautiful just the way you are.

(Rupert thought that one was the cheesiest.)

Okay, so his mother wasn't very good at her third job, but it was difficult for her to support him on her own, so Rupert did his best to be encouraging.

Rupert turned around a sharp bend in the road. He began to climb a set of steep and narrow stairs, a shortcut that led straight home. He fantasized about how he'd walk through the foyer. His mother would give him a hug and tell him that he'd never have to go back to Mrs. Frabbleknacker's class ever again if he didn't want to.

Of course, that would never happen. More likely, she would be upset that he was out and about near the witchy parts of town so close to dusk.

But Rupert knew he wasn't the only one who was interested in the witches. Last year, Kaleigh came into school on her tenth birthday proudly wearing a brooch that she had gotten from a witch shop. Hal's family loved to walk through the witchy streets; he talked about it all the time. Kyle went on a broomstick ride above Gliverstoll with his younger brother in the beginning of the year. Bruno claimed that his mother had been severely allergic to nuts, dairy, gluten, strawberries, soy, eggs, seafood, legumes, latex, dust mites, and pollen, but the witches sold her potions that cured all her allergies right up. And Allison swore that her mother's rose garden blossomed because of all the care the witches took in the town.

But when Rupert tried to tell his mother all the nice things his friends had said about the witches, she refused to listen. In fact, every time Rupert mentioned the witches, his mother grimaced and reminded him to stay far, far away from the witches.

But he always wondered: What was the point of living in one of the only witch towns left if he couldn't ever see a witch?

. . . .

The Great and Terrible Things About Mothers

THE GREAT THING ABOUT MOTHERS IS THAT THEY are always there to comfort you and clean you when you come home reeking of sewage.

The Terrible Thing About Mothers is that they never believe you when you try to tell them about evil teachers who make you dig in garbage for a paper clip.

"Oh, what a wild imagination," they say. "Now stop playing in trash. It's dirty. There are germs. . . ." And then they drone on and on for hours about tiny bacteria and microorganisms and the benefits of antibacterial soap.

Rupert frowned as he listened to his mother's germ rant.

After the stern talking-to, Rupert's mother ushered him into the tub and shoved him under the water, clothes and all. Then she took a washcloth and scrubbed his arms where the mud caked his skin.

"Mom," Rupert said. "I'm eleven years old. I can do it myself."

His mother *tsk*ed. That was not a good sign.

"Rupert Archibald Campbell, obviously you don't make good choices if you decided that the best way to spend your afternoon was rolling around in the dirt like a pig."

"It wasn't my choice—Mrs. Frabbleknacker made me do it."

His mother shook her head disapprovingly. "Not this nonsense again."

"It's not nonsense, Mom!" Rupert insisted. "She's really evil. Super evil."

"The only thing that's super evil around here is your stench. Now, you need to take responsibility for your own actions."

"But Mrs. Frabbleknacker hid a paper clip in a dump, and she wouldn't let us leave until someone found it!"

His mother laughed. "Oh, Rupert, you have the

wildest imagination. Sometimes I wonder where you come up with such stories."

Rupert sunk down in the tub in defeat. He started thinking about a conversation he'd had with Allison Gormley, Kyle Mason-Reed, and Hal Porter a few months ago, back when Mrs. Frabbleknacker let her students talk to each other. Hal and Allison had mentioned that their parents wouldn't believe them when they tried to tell them about Mrs. Frabbleknacker's horrible lessons. Their parents had just laughed, too—and then patted them on their heads and sent them outside to play. Why was it so hard to get their parents to believe them? *There must be some universal, understood code among all parents that makes them think their kids are always making up stories or telling jokes,* Rupert thought.

"Don't worry," his mother said. "I'm almost done with you. I just want to get this muck off your arms, now that I've started scrubbing. Then I promise I'll leave you alone. What do you want for dinner—pizza? I'll even let you eat in the tub." She winked at him.

"I think I'll take it in my room, please," Rupert said. He didn't want to think about dropping a slice of pizza in the grimy bathwater, but his mind instantly went there. He knew that if Mrs. Frabbleknacker were here, she would make him *eat* the bathwater pizza, and that was an even worse thought.

"I can give you microwavable pizza, microwavable lasagna, microwavable quesadillas, microwavable popcorn, microwavable rice, microwavable chocolate soufflé, microwavable cheese, microwavable toast, or microwavable cheese on toast. Which do you prefer?"

Rupert groaned. "Does everything in our house *have* to be microwavable?"

"Oh, Rupert, you know I'm too exhausted to cook by the time I get home from work."

"So, how was work today?"

Rupert's mother hummed absently. "The day was lovely. Except . . . " She froze and looked at nothing in particular with glazed, distant eyes. "Mrs. Marmalin had to chase a witch out of the quilting shop with a broom."

Rupert nodded. "I ran into Mrs. Marmalin on the way up here. She told me." His mother wrung out the dirty washcloth in the sink. "What did the witch look like? What did she say? Did she do any spells? Did she hex you?"

His mother laughed.

"I just can't believe you actually met a witch. I mean—I've obviously seen the pack flying around Gliverstoll, but I've never talked to one!"

"And let's hope you never have to," his mother said with a shudder. "Remember what I said about the witches, Rupert. This one in particular had a downright dreadful temper. She kept calling herself the 'Queen of the Sea,' and threatened to slap us with a dead fish."

"Cool! Then what happened?"

"Rupert!" his mother said, in a scolding sort of voice. "I will not indulge your curiosity! I've told you a thousand times: stay away from the witches—"

"But why?"

"They are dangerous! And horrible! And terrible!"

"Why? What's wrong with them?"

"Wisdom is just another word for obedience," his mother said, reciting a fortune cookie.

"Didn't you tell me last week that another word for genius is obsession?"

"Rupert!"

Rupert folded his arms. "All right, all right. I'll stay away from the witches."

There was a long pause, and Rupert hoped his mother had let the subject drop.

His mother finally put the grimy washcloth on the bathroom floor and stood up. "I suppose that's as good as I'm going to get. I'm leaving so you can take a real bath." His mother turned to leave the bathroom, but then she paused with her hand on the doorknob. "Rupert, why don't I see any of your friends around the house anymore? Did something happen? Are you fighting?"

Rupert frowned. Now that his mother mentioned it, the loneliness seemed real. And it all boiled down to Mrs. Frabbleknacker. She was the horrible, rotten reason that none of them talked to him anymore—because she forbid them to talk before class, she forbid them to talk during class, and she forbid them to talk after class.

"Everything's fine," Rupert lied. "We're just really busy, now that we're in fifth grade."

His mother sniffled. "My little boy is growing up!" And with the soft creak of the closing door, she was gone.

Rupert watched the dirt swirl around in the bathwater. Dirt and grime. Grime and dirt. Rupert churned it with his finger. When he got bored, he hung his body over the side of the bathtub, thinking about what had happened. Millie Michaels found the paper clip—but then Mrs. Frabbleknacker made her stay while the rest of the class got to go. Poor Millie. She thought she had won the lottery, only to have the rules changed.

Rupert leaned forward out of the bathtub, accidentally dripping water everywhere as he grabbed the newspaper that was sitting in the rack beside the toilet. He flipped right to the comics section for a bit of cheering up, but on the adjacent page, a notice in the classified section caught his eye:

WITCH NEEDS

One apprentice. Tasks include testing potions and other things. Skill sets for applicants should include intelligence and other things. Applicants should be children preferably. Don't worry—will not make Toecorn out of you (this witch finds Toecorn much less appetizing than Knuckle Soup).

Rabbits need not apply.

Rupert tore the article out of the paper. Then he folded it and placed it in the sole of his shoe.

A witch's apprentice. As he thought about the job, excitement bubbled in his stomach (or maybe that was the dump sludge finally catching up with him).

This was perfect. Beyond perfect. The most perfectly perfectest perfecty thing to ever fall beside Rupert's toilet.

Rupert's Interview

ON SATURDAY—AFTER RUPERT'S MOTHER LEFT for work—Rupert changed into his very best suit and tie for his job interview. He was to meet the witch in Digglydare Close, a stuffy alleyway at sea level.

As Rupert left his house, he was thinking about how far up the mountain he lived. On the one hand, Rupert loved the beautiful view of the ocean from his window, but on the other hand, Main Beach was quite a hike down the hill. Today, Rupert wasn't particularly excited to schlep all the way to Digglydare Close, which was right off Main Beach.

Rupert crossed the street diagonally to get to the

top of the staircase that cut through the town and led all the way down the hill. The steps were quite narrow, winding, and steep, and Rupert had to hold onto the broken stone walls of the stairs all the way down. Even climbing down the steps was a workout, and when Rupert finally reached the Main Beach at the bottom, he wiped his sweaty forehead with his sleeve.

He stared at the Main Beach, a small area of grainy sand that connected to the endless ocean. The water glowed a neon shade of blue, and the smell of the salty seawater was so strong that Rupert could almost taste it. He had heard tourists complain about the stench, but this fishy tang smelled like home to him.

Rupert walked through the beach to the shops that lined the bottom of the rocky hill. A few local shopkeepers waved in Rupert's direction, and Mrs. Gummyum, the owner of the ice-cream store where his mother worked, called out to him.

"Rupert!" she said, waddling over to him. "Where's our favorite ice-cream taster today?"

"You mean Mom? She's working at the . . ." he was about to spill his mother's fortune-cookie secret.

"Working on learning how to cook," he said, which was a terribly unconvincing lie to anyone who knew his mother at all.

"Cook?" Mrs. Gummyum said. "Cook! Why does she need to cook when she can eat all of my ice-cream flavors? She's not trying to make ice cream, is she? Not that we couldn't handle a competing store—"

"Mom's not cooking ice cream, Mrs. Gummyum," Rupert reassured her. "She's making vegetables."

"Vegetables? Who needs vegetables? Unless you're making spinach and artichoke ice cream, the only vegetable ice cream around. Though lately I've been dreaming of carrot ice cream . . . perhaps I should try that . . ."

"She's cooking vegetables for my health. I'm a growing boy," he said, which is something that every adult had said to him for as long as he could remember. "But anyway, Mrs. Gummyum, I have to go. I'm late!"

"Late for what? Late—oh, that gives me a marvelous idea! What do you think of Time-of-the-Day Ice Cream, Rupert? Like Day-of-the-Week Undergarments, only much better. There'll be an ice cream for every hour, minute, and second. Think about it—that's at least five thousand new ice creams, all rolled into one idea."

"Sorry! Truly sorry—gotta run!" Rupert ran off before he could get caught in another one of her long-winded ice-cream suggestions.

Rupert looked at his watch as he jogged through the town—his delay with Mrs. Gummyum left him two minutes late, and he dashed past a store of knickknacks, the quilting store, a candy store, and a jack-in-the-box emporium. At the very end of the strip, Rupert passed Cats, Rats, Bats, and Hats: A Witch's Top Shop and Broomstick Tours: Showing You Gliverstoll on the Fly, two of the witchy businesses in Gliverstoll that generated money and tourists for the town.

At last, Rupert finally arrived at Digglydare Close, and he peered into the shadowy street. He saw no one.

Maybe the witch had decided she didn't want an apprentice after all. Maybe he would never find her—maybe he would never be able to talk to anyone ever again.

Rupert walked through the Close. "Hello? Anyone there?"

A breeze wooshed and swooshed through the alleyway. He heard a cackle, which turned into a throaty cough. Rupert followed the noise down an intersecting alleyway, and he kept following the sound until he stood in front of a wooden door on Pexale Close. The coughs were definitely coming from the other side of the door.

Rupert looked around the cobblestone path. Was he supposed to follow the cackling coughs? Or was he supposed to wait for the witch at Digglydare Close? Should he turn around? Or should he go in?

Rupert knocked on the door. It swung open, and he slinked into a musty room that smelled like a sweaty shoe. The room was filled with shelves, stacked top to bottom with books, bottles, and odd knickknacks, but Rupert was more focused on a hunched figure that stood over a cauldron. The figure looked to be brewing a potion, and even in the darkness, Rupert saw her pointy teeth gleaming in a wicked grin.

He instantly regretted coming to meet her. What if she cooked his toes into Toecorn? What if she boiled his fingers into Knuckle Soup? Or squeezed his eyeballs for jelly? How could he possibly have been so stupid and so careless? If he disappeared, no one would ever know what happened to him. He should have taken his mother's cell phone or left a note on the kitchen counter . . . or had some sort of contingency plan.

Rupert looked up at her, his knees knocking. "H-hello," he said. He tried to smile as pleasantly as possible, but he was sure it looked more like a grimace.

"Are you here for the interview?" the witch croaked, her voice low and crackly.

Rupert nodded.

The witch leaned forward into the slices of daylight that snuck in from the window shades. In the dim light, Rupert saw the woman's gigantic, crooked, warty, grandflubbing nose, and he saw her rotten, daggerly teeth. The woman raised a gnobbled hand toward Rupert and pointed at the seat.

"Sit."

Rupert took a seat, looking down at the witch's feet. But then he noticed she had no feet at all—just four wooden pegs that came out from under her cloak. Rupert looked up at the witch's green-ish face, realizing that her face was greener in some places than others and that her face looked awfully splotchy. And there was a thin lining of plastic around her nose.

He squinted and leaned closer. Rupert thought he saw—yes! The witch was wearing costume makeup!

Rupert snickered. But he didn't want to be rude, so he bit his lips and blew his cheeks out, desperately trying to swallow his laughter. His eyes bugged, and his face turned red.

"Oh!" the witch gasped. "He's having a fit!" She rushed forward to help him, but she tripped on the robe that was several feet too long for her, and she fell splat on the floor. Her prosthetic nose popped off, flew into the air, and landed in the cauldron with a hiss.

Rupert howled until tears were leaking out of his eyes. "I'm sorry—I shouldn't laugh," he wheezed.

The witch fished her fake nose out of the cauldron with a ladle, but the piece of plastic had completely melted into rubbery goo.

"That was my best nose, too," she said sadly.

She snapped her fingers and the lights turned on. In the brightness of the room, Rupert could clearly see where the witch tried to smudge green makeup on her face and where she had stuck on a plastic nose. She reached into her mouth and removed her set of false pointy dentures. Without the fake teeth, the witch had a row of normal square teeth, just like everyone else Rupert had ever met.

The witch pulled the wig of long black hair off her head and then wiped her face on a towel until most of the green makeup was off. She still had a greenish hue to her, but Rupert was sure that the rest of the makeup would come off with a good shower. At last, the witch popped off her fake hands.

Without her makeup and her prosthetic append-ages, she had freckly skin, pale yellow hair, a tiny nose, and round baby-faced cheeks. She was a lot shorter than Rupert would have imagined her—and a lot younger. Rupert thought she looked about his age.

"You aren't really a witch, are you?" Rupert asked.

"Course I am," the girl said.

"Then why are you wearing all of that makeup?"

She sighed. "I don't suppose you would know anything about it. I haven't grown into my nose, hands, and height yet. And I'm not old enough for nose warts. But if I want to be a real witch someday I have to start acting like one now. Hold on—*I'm* interviewing *you*. Not the other way around. So from now on, I'll be asking the questions."

The witch dug an old-fashioned tape recorder out of her pocket and placed it on the table.

The interview transcript:

The witch: What is your name?

Rupert: Rupert Campbell.

The witch: How old are you?

Rupert: I'm eleven.

The witch: Why, you're just a baby!

Rupert: Well, how old are you?

The witch: I'm twelve.

Rupert: *(snorting sounds)*

The witch: Are you smart?

Rupert: I think so.

The witch: What's two plus three?

Rupert: Five.

The witch: Pity. I thought I asked for smart applicants.

Rupert: That's the right answer!

The witch: What's five plus monkey?

Rupert: Five plus monkey? What in the world does that mean?

The witch: Wrong. Giraffe.

Rupert: Giraffe what?

The witch: Now what's five plus ape?

Rupert: Jellyfish?

The witch: Wrong again. It's thirteen.

Rupert: No, five plus *eight* is thirteen. Eight, not ape.

The witch: Wrong again. Five plus eight is kangaroo. Now what's two plus three?

Rupert: Honeybee.

The witch: *(scribbles on a paper)* Well at least you are a quick learner. Now . . . are you a bunny?

Rupert: A bunny?

The witch: Are you? Answer honestly!

Rupert: No, I'm a boy.

The witch: A boy bunny?

Rupert: No, no! Just a boy. A human boy.

The witch: You can never be too careful these days. *(scribbles on a paper)*

End of transcript.

The witch looked at Rupert with her eyebrows raised, and Rupert couldn't tell whether this was a good omen or a bad one. He started to feel a bit squirmy, and so he stuck his hands in his pockets to calm his nerves. The witch stared at him some more, and Rupert had a horrible feeling that she was considering brewing his fingers into Knuckle Soup.

"Thank you for coming out to meet me," she said with a wave of her hand, "now good-bye."

"What, that's it?" Rupert said. "What about the part where we talk about my qualifications? And why I want this job? And my future ambitions?" He knew all about job interviews, since his mom had been on so many, and he had prepared thoroughly.

The witch drummed her fingers on the table. "Fine then, what are your qualifications? Have you ever worked with a witch before?"

"Well, no but I—"

"Then you have no qualifications."

Rupert could almost feel the job slipping away from him. "I'm—I'm a hard worker! Just give me a chance!"

"Anything else?" the witch said, looking bored.

"Why do you want an apprentice anyway?"

The witch put her hands on her hips. "That's for me to know and you to never find out. Now, if you have no more questions, then you may go."

"But—"

"Go now," the girl said. "Before I bake you into pudding."

Rupert kicked the ground. "Thank you for your time," he mumbled.

He stumbled out the door, his cheeks growing hot. How could he have botched the interview so badly? He insulted her, couldn't answer a single one of her questions, and then had no qualifications for the job. He climbed the steps up to his house, certain he would never hear from the witch again.

The Chase

THE NEXT MORNING, THE PHONE RANG.

"Hello, I'd like to speak to . . . Rupert Campbell please."

"This is he."

"Hi, Rupert, this is . . . erm . . . the witch. I'd like to offer you the job. What do you say?"

Rupert nodded vigorously, too stunned to find his voice.

"Erm . . . hello?" the witch said. "Darn these stupid things—Storm, the phone is broken again! I can't hear a thing!"

Rupert heard a voice in the background, shouting: "Smack it on the table! Stupid mortal devices—give it a good thump on the rump!"

"Don't!" Rupert shouted. "You'll only break the phone!"

He heard a crack, and then the witch said, "Oh, there you are! Oh, no, there you *were*. Now there are lots of loud fuzzy noises."

"That's because you're not supposed to thump phones on the rump!" Rupert said.

"CAN YOU HEAR ME?"

Rupert pulled the phone away from his ear. "Ow! Stop yelling!"

"WITCH TO BOY, WITCH TO BOY—CAN YOU HEAR ME? IF YOU CAN HEAR ME, START WORK IN ONE HOUR. MEET AT THE FISHING DOCK. WEAR PURPLE. IF YOU CAN'T HEAR ME, THEN MEET ME AT MAIN BEACH IN TWO HOURS, AND WEAR ORANGE."

Rupert shook his head. How would he know to meet her at Main Beach if he couldn't hear her?

"THIS IS FUN! LA LA LA! DO YOU EVER NOTICE THAT WORDS SOUND FUNNY IF YOU SAY THEM TOO MANY TIMES? ESPECIALLY WORM. WORM. WORM. WORM, WORM, WORM. WORM, WORM, WORM, WORM, WORM-WORM-WORM. ACTUALLY,

BRING LOLLIPOPS TO THE FISHING DOCK!"

There was a click, and the dial tone started again.

Rupert's mother walked in the room with the clean laundry and set it on the kitchen table. She danced around the kitchen table and wiggled her butt, doing what she called a "funky little boogie dance," and Rupert laughed. Watching her reminded him of all the times he used to dance around the kitchen with her when he was younger. She used to grab him under the armpits and swing him up onto the kitchen table, where he would dance until he was out of breath. Then he would count to three before jumping from the table. His mother always caught him and spun him around in circles. That is, before she was too busy to do anything but work.

His mother stopped dancing and winked at him.

"Who was that on the phone?" she asked, folding Rupert's shirt.

"No one," Rupert said. He tried to lie smoothly, but he could feel his cheeks and neck growing red.

His mother raised one eyebrow. Rupert was always amazed at the way she was able to raise just her left one. No matter how hard he practiced in the mirror, he could never quite get it to look right.

Whenever he tried, he ended up looking like a scrunched up meatball.

Rupert looked his mother in the eye, his heart racing. "It was just Kaleigh," he said. "From school. She got bored and wanted to talk. That's all."

"I don't believe you," his mother said. "I know you better than you know yourself, and I know you know that I know you're lying. I don't know what you're up to, Rupert, but when I find out, I better like it."

"You won't find out, so you won't have to," Rupert muttered, dumping his empty cereal bowl in the sink.

A half hour later, Rupert set out for the fishing dock, wearing purple and carrying lollipops.

The witch was lying stomach-down on the dock, her face just above the water. Her blond hair was tied up in a very high ponytail that rested almost at the top of her head, and Rupert thought she looked especially unwitch-like in her short white pants and pink tank top. In fact, she looked just like any normal girl.

The dock creaked under Rupert's feet, and the witch turned around to hush him. Rupert tiptoed the rest of the way.

"Get down," she hissed, and Rupert obeyed.

With his face near the water, Rupert asked, "What are we looking for?"

"Here, fishy fishy fishy!" the witch called. "Come here you cute widdle fishy!"

"Are we trying to catch a fish?"

The witch turned to him, her eyes wide in horror. "Shhh! They have ears, Rupert! You'll scare them away!"

Rupert laughed. "Well, you'll never catch a fish like that! You think a fish is going to come running when you call it?"

"Why not?" the witch asked defensively. "My cat comes when I call it!"

"This is a fish," Rupert said, shaking his head. "F-I-S—" But before he could finish spelling the word, the witch made kissy noises, and hundreds of fish leaped out of the water. Rupert had never seen anything like it—it was like jumping trout or leaping salmon or mini-dolphins—it was utterly amazing.

The witch reached out and grabbed a fish just before it descended into water, and Rupert looked at her with his mouth agape.

"I suppose you've never gone fishing either?" the

witch said. "What a useless apprentice I've taken on!"

She started to walk away, and Rupert scrambled to keep up.

"Why am I wearing purple?" he said. "Does this have to do with some spell you're going to do?"

The witch shrugged. "No, I just like the color purple."

"And what about these lollipops?"

The witch snatched them out of his hands and popped three in her mouth. Her cheeks bulged like an overstuffed coin purse.

"I WUV WOWWYPOPS," she hummed, and continued walking.

Rupert ran after her. She blew past Digglydare Close, and to Rupert's surprise, she blew past Pexale Close, too. Rupert tried to ask her where they were going, but she put a finger to her lips and shook her head.

Rupert's stomach did a kick. He had the oddest feeling—like something bad was following him—but when he turned to look over his shoulder, he saw nothing there.

Rupert caught up to the witch and took a sideways look at her face. She looked nervous, too. Rupert couldn't help feeling that her wobbly expression was somehow related to his feeling of being followed. But when he took a breath to ask her about what was happening, the witch clamped her hand over his mouth.

"Mmmm!" Rupert said.

"I think they're on to us!"

"Mmmm?"

"The Fairfoul Witch, that's who!"

"Mmmm mmmm?"

"My lair must have been booby-trapped for humans. I could smell the magic when we got close," the witch said. She let go of his mouth and grabbed his hand instead. She pulled him up the stairs that led away from the beach and up to the roads and restaurants of Gliverstoll.

"Oh, I knew I shouldn't have put that ad in the newspaper," she groaned. "And I shouldn't have hung up flyers. And I definitely shouldn't have stood on the beach with a megaphone."

The witch leaped up, skipping steps. Rupert ran after her, but then his side started to ache, and he panted for breath.

"Come *on*, Rupert!" she said. "We have to get out of here, now!"

Rupert coughed and panted, and the witch paced back and forth on the steps above.

"Ah!" she said. "Okay." She closed her eyes, and when she opened them she looked fiercely behind Rupert. "I need to get this boy to move faster," she said.

Rupert looked behind him, but no one was there. Who was this witch talking to?

"I need a Jetpack," she said, and she snapped her fingers.

CRACK.

In a blink, the witch held a brown over-the-shoulder bag with a zipper on top and holes on the sides.

"Is the Jetpack in there?" Rupert said.

The witch shook her head. "It-it's not a Jetpack," she said in a very small voice. "It's a pet sack."

"A pet sack?"

"A pet sack."

"But we need a *Jetpack.*"

"They're getting closer," the witch said.

"Who?" Rupert asked, turning to look behind him again. Still, nothing.

"The witches . . . the Witches Council. The Fair-foul Witch and all her underlings."

"Well, *you're* a witch!" Rupert said. "Can't you stop them?"

The witch opened the pet sack. "This can work. Get in."

"You want *me* to get in *there?*" Rupert grabbed the pet sack. It was made for a medium-sized dog—or perhaps a giant cat. It couldn't possibly fit an average-sized boy like him.

"Yes!" the witch said. "And hurry!"

Rupert zipped open the bag and curled himself inside. He contorted in a way he didn't think he possibly could. Somehow his ankle was by his ear and his wrists were knocking his knees—and his head popped out of the bag just slightly. The witch threw the bag over her shoulder and darted up the stairs. Rupert marveled at her speed—even while carrying him over her shoulder, she was just as fast.

With every landing, Rupert thumped against the witch's side, which hurt his twisted-up body, but he tried not to think about it. Instead he peered out of the bag, watching for the top of the stairs. They were so close! Then Rupert turned around to look behind them.

This time, he caught a glimpse of the witches.

There were about ten of them chasing them up the stairs. Some pointed crooked, gnobbly fingers in Rupert's direction. Others let out menacing cackles. Rupert gulped and ducked back into his pet sack.

"They're behind us!" he said.

"Don't you think I know that?" the witch shouted. "Hold on! It's about to get bumpy—"

And she leaped up the stairs so fast that Rupert thought she was flying—she skipped twenty steps and landed with a *THUMP* just before the top step. The witch flung the bag that held Rupert onto her other shoulder, and she sprinted toward the residential area.

A Lie, the Witches Council, and the Bar Exam

"WHERE ARE WE GOING?" RUPERT ASKED.

"Trust me," the witch said, stopping at the park.

The witch ran over to a sandbox, dropped Rupert gently in the sand, and sat down next to him. She snapped both her fingers, and the sand flew up around the edges of the sandbox. Then it converged together above their heads; they were stuck in a sand dome.

"Won't this be a little obvious?" Rupert said. "A giant sand bubble in the middle of the playground?"

"Witches have eyesight that is five times better than the best human, but they have trouble seeing sand," the witch said. "Well, they can see it, but it's slippery on their eyes."

"Slippery?"

"It's like when you're walking in a crowded street. You certainly see other people—but can you tell me what they look like? It's because your eyes just see them and slip off. I have narwhal-narwhal vision, and even *I* have trouble seeing it. The only reason I'm better at this is because my eyes are younger and stronger."

"It's unfortunate that you settled near a beach, then."

"Long story," the witch said.

Rupert, still crouched in the pet sack, scratched his ear with his toe.

"Hey, what's your name?" Rupert said. "If I'm working for you now, I should call you something."

The witch bit her lip. "I . . . well . . ." she stammered. "I don't have a name."

"Don't have a name!" Rupert said, aghast.

The witch's lip began to quiver. "Oh, Rupert! I lied to you! I told you I was a witch, but I'm not! Not yet."

"Yes you are!" Rupert said. "I never would have believed it from the way you dress, but I've seen you do magic. I'm twisted up in a pet sack for goodness sakes!"

"I'm not a *real* witch yet. I'm just a witchling. That's why I need an apprentice—to help me practice for my Bar Exam."

"Bar Exam?"

"Yes . . . that is my witch test. It's coming up in four weeks. I become part of the Council once I pass my exam—and then I'll be a full-fledged witch, and I'll finally get to pick my name."

"Pick it?"

"Of course. That's the best part, silly. Until then, I guess you can call me Witchling Two. That's what Nebby and Storm call me."

Rupert raised his eyebrows. "And who are Nebby and Storm?"

"They're my witch guardians, silly! The Nebulous Witch and the Storm Witch."

Rupert scrunched his face. "Who?"

Witchling Two stuck her finger in the sand. She wrote THE WITCHES COUNCIL in big, swoopy cursive. Then underneath, she wrote:

Top Witch:
    THE FAIRFOUL WITCH

The Undercat:
>   THE MIDNIGHT WITCH

Council of Three:
>   THE LIGHTNING WITCH
>   THE THUNDER WITCH
>   THE STORM WITCH

The Underbelly:
>   THE STONE WITCH
>   THE NEBULOUS WITCH
>   THE HIBBLY WITCH
>   THE COLDWIND WITCH
>   THE SEA WITCH

Witchlings (not technically Witches Council ... yet!):
>   WITCHLING ONE
>   WITCHLING TWO (ME!)
>   WITCHLING THREE
>   WITCHLING FOUR
>   WITCHLING FIVE

"Make sense?" Witchling Two said.

Rupert shook his head no. "Not even a little bit."

"Okay. So the Fairfoul Witch is the top witch. The head honcho. The cherry on the sundae, the cheese on the nachos, the sauce on the pasta—"

"I get it," Rupert interrupted.

"She is in charge of the Witches Council, and everyone has to listen to her. She is the strongest and oldest witch."

"I've read about her," Rupert admitted. "She's the only witch anyone ever writes about in the papers."

"That's because she's the boss."

"So no one ever crosses her?"

"Exactly. And she has an Undercat, named the Midnight Witch. She's really scary, too, but not half as terrifying as the Fairfoul Witch. The Midnight Witch has been dying to overthrow the Fairfoul Witch for ages. Everyone knows it—she tries to get rid of the Fairfoul Witch all the time."

"And the Fairfoul Witch doesn't get mad?"

Witchling Two shook her head no. "She thinks it's amusing. The Fairfoul Witch knows it will take centuries of practice before the Midnight Witch is powerful enough to actually beat her."

Rupert pointed to the Council of Three. "What's that?"

"The Council of Three answers to the Midnight

Witch. Then the Underbelly consists of young witches."

"How young?"

"The youngest one is eighty."

Rupert's eyes bugged out. "Eighty!"

Witchling Two nodded. "Since they're relatively new, they just get to vote on things. They're kind of the bottom of the heap. But each member of the Underbelly gets her own witchling to raise."

"So you belong to the Nebulous Witch?" Rupert said, pointing to Witchling Two's chart.

"Yes. And the Nebulous Witch used to belong to the Storm Witch back before the Storm Witch got promoted to the Council of Three. So in a way, Storm is . . . she's the human equivalent of my grandfather."

"Grand*mother*."

"Yes—Godbrother. That's what I said."

Rupert rolled his eyes.

"But how are the Undercat, Council of Three, and the Underbelly chosen?"

"Well it mostly goes in age order—the oldest witches have seniority, so they get the better positions. The younger witches just have to wait."

If the youngest witch was eighty, Rupert couldn't even imagine how old the oldest witch must be. Rupert stared at Witchling Two's chart, looking at all the witches. And then he suddenly got embarrassed. He didn't want to ask, but he couldn't help but notice that there were only *women* witches.

"Can you tell me," he said sheepishly, "where baby witches come from?"

"Oh, the same place human babies come from," she said. "From an egg."

"An *egg*?" Rupert snorted.

Witchling Two nodded. "In Witch Primary School, I had a class on humans. I know all about how they work. The mommy human lays an egg and has to sit on it for three years. Then a human hatches."

Rupert opened his mouth to correct her, but then he didn't really see the point.

"Er . . . good thing you have primary school then," Rupert said.

"Definitely!" Witchling Two said, nodding vigorously.

Rupert stared at the Witches Council list that Witchling Two drew in the sand. She was number two out of five witchlings. The more Rupert thought about this, the more confused he became. Until he finally asked, "Why did you contact a human? There are four other witchlings training for their exam, right? Why wouldn't you just ask *them* for help?"

"Erm . . . well . . . the other witches were all too busy," she said quickly. "So, I thought I'd get help from a human instead."

"But I can't help you with magic," Rupert said.

"Sure you can." She patted Rupert's head, which was still sticking out of the pet sack. "I have a potions book, and so you can help me brew. And you can quiz me on magic, even if you can't do it yourself. Here—ask me to conjure something up."

"How about you conjure me out of this pet sack?"

"What?" Witchling Two said. "I didn't catch that."

"Conjure me a chocolate milkshake with a very long, bendable straw."

Witchling Two snapped her fingers. "Milkshake," she breathed. "Milkshake."

CRACK.

The ground mumbled and rumbled and grumbled. Then it groaned and moaned. The Earth splintered beneath Rupert—the sand underneath him began to jerk. Then his pet sack popped up to the top of the sand dome and Rupert face-planted into the ground. He swallowed a mouthful of sand.

"An earthquake!" Rupert choked, spitting the sand out of his mouth. "I asked for a milkshake!"

"I told you I need practice!" Witchling Two shouted.

"Well *do* something! If you don't stop this earthquake, the sand bubble will break, and the witches will find us!"

"I know!" Witchling Two said between gritted teeth. Rupert saw a bead of sweat trickle down her round face. Witchling Two snapped her fingers. The ground still shook. Then she snapped her fingers again and again. She snapped about a thousand times before the ground quieted and fell still.

"Was that you?" Rupert breathed. "Did you stop it?"

Witchling Two shook her head. "To be honest, I think the earthquake just ran its course."

"And how long do we have to stay in the sand?"

Witchling Two whistled, long and low. "I don't know," she said. "I didn't intend for the Council to find out about you, but somehow they did. And now you're in terrible danger."

"Danger?" Rupert said. "What danger?"

"A witch has never asked a human for help before! And now the Witches Council is after you, and it's all my fault!"

She started to sniffle, and he didn't know what to do to console her. He thought maybe he should pat her on the back, but he was still all twisted up inside the pet sack, so he settled on awkwardly rubbing his head against her arm. "There, there," he said.

She mussed his hair. "You're lucky you were in the pet sack—they didn't see your face right?"

Rupert nodded. Maybe they saw the top of his head when he peeked out from the pet sack, but there were lots of people in Gliverstoll with light brown hair. They would never recognize him from his hair alone.

"That's good," Witchling Two said. "I'm sure you've heard terrible stories about witches, right? I thought it was a bit surprising that you answered my Classified Ad. You're the only human who responded—that's why I thought you were a bunny in disguise."

"I've heard stories about the witches—I just didn't think they were as terrible as everyone makes them seem."

Witchling Two shook her head. "Oh no, they're worse! I've watched them do horrendous things. Once I saw them make a boy eat his way out of a pool full of Jell-O."

Rupert paused. "Actually," he said after a moment's thought, "that doesn't sound so bad."

"Talk to me after you've eaten two thousand, three hundred, and fifty-two cubic feet of Jell-O. That poor boy could hardly walk. His stomach was so big and plushy that his sisters tried to use him as a trampoline for weeks."

"So that's what they would do to me if they found me? Make me eat myself to death?"

"Maybe," Witchling Two said. "Or maybe not. They're particularly fond of making people lick the dead skin off their feet."

Rupert made a face.

"One thing's for sure though—you won't be found. I may be a mediocre witch—"

"A horrible witch," Rupert muttered under his breath.

"—And you might just be a normal boy. But I still need your help to pass my exam, and now you need my help to stay alive."

"Alive?" Rupert gulped.

Witchling Two stood up and popped her head through the top of the sand bubble, which—when she was standing up fully—was as tall as her neck. Then, she ran through the sand bubble until it started to crumble.

"What are you doing?" Rupert asked.

"Popping the bubble! The witches are gone. We're safe now!"

She skipped around the sandbox until the bubble was entirely destroyed. Rupert shook his head to get the lumps of sand off. A few grains got in his eyes and he teared up as he tried to blink them out.

"Are you crying?" Witchling Two said as she picked up the pet sack. "I learned in primary school that humans only cry when they are extremely happy." Rupert tried to correct her, but Witchling Two began to sob. "This is so great!" she blubbered, her tears flying everywhere, as she walked toward his house. "I am so happy, too, Rupert—I've never had a human friend before!"

The Warning

THE NEXT DAY, RUPERT SET OFF FOR A TEA SHOP called The Brewery on Digglydare Close. Rupert had never been to The Brewery before, even though he had seen it. The Brewery was past an invisible line that his mother drew on the south side of town. He felt a little guilty walking there because he knew his mother wouldn't approve, but the tea shop wasn't even owned by any witches. Besides, he would be with a friend who would protect him.

Luckily, when he left, his mother was out taste testing for Mrs. Gummyum, so he didn't have to explain anything to her.

The sea wind was a bit nippier than normal, but he enjoyed the crisp breeze as he hustled through town.

He arrived at The Brewery a little early, so he sat at a table by the window while he waited. He stared outside and had the most spectacular view of the sea as it rocked the boats docked by the shore. Then he looked at the sand, which was shining and sparkling in the sunlight. The beach was packed with tourists. He could tell because of all the cameras. Plus, plenty of them had witch-themed towels and umbrellas, which Rupert knew they bought at the biggest tourist trap of all: Witchknack: Trinket and Novelty Store.

Rupert spotted Kaleigh at the beach with her family. Over by the rocks, a few people were lying out in the sand. There was almost nobody actually swimming today, probably because of the overcast sky—

THUMP.

Rupert jumped.

Witchling Two had thwapped a book the size of four dictionaries on the table.

"What in the world is *that*?" Rupert said.

"Oh, just your routine textbook."

"I'm not going to have to read all that, am I?"

"Do you want to?" she said excitedly. "Here!" She opened up to page 1482.

Rupert bent over the text.

Spells should be enunciated assuredly from the vessel; cogitation must linger on the vocation at hand; onus of liability is on the caster; no quid pro quos except in a duel with an allochthonous witch, in which a mutually agreed upon exchange must be made agreeable to the entire clans of all parties involved.

"What does this mean?" Rupert groaned.

"Sounds like there are going to be parties!" Witchling Two said, clapping her hands together.

Somehow, he didn't think that was it. "Does it go on for thousands of pages like this?"

Witchling Two nodded. "I've got a few other textbooks at home. Should I bring those next time?"

"No!" Rupert shouted. The people at the next table gave him a strange look, and he lowered his voice. "At the very least, let's order breakfast. Then we can try to understand your textbook."

They walked up to the counter and looked at the menu behind the coffee machines. Rupert ordered a cheese omelet. Witchling Two ordered poached eggs, bacon, ham, mash, buttered toast, a slice of quiche, a large pot of tea, two scones, one biscuit, one piece of shortbread, and four lollipops from the jar by the cashier.

"Hungry?" Rupert asked.

"Not really. Why?"

"Nothing," Rupert said, walking back over to their table.

Rupert climbed back into the booth, and Witchling Two jumped into the seat across from him, but with the book on the table, Rupert couldn't even see her face. He only saw her ponytail. Rupert stood up and pushed the book to the other end of the table, using all the strength he could muster.

"Now I can see your face," he explained.

"Goody! But you should probably slide the book back over here."

"Why?"

"You still have to explain what it says."

"But there are five thousand pages!" Rupert protested. "Maybe more!"

Witchling Two nodded. "I've been trying to understand it for years, which is why I'm so glad I have you, Rupert!"

"But if you've been reading it for years, how am I supposed to understand it in a few minutes?"

Witchling Two shrugged.

Rupert frowned. "Then, why don't you train with

the other witches or witchlings? Surely they'd be better than me."

"But you are so . . . um . . . specially spectacular, Rupert. Your . . . er . . . creative mind sets you leagues above the witches." She hesitated.

"I don't believe you," Rupert said.

But before he had a chance to press her anymore about it, the waitress came with their food. Witchling Two tore into her poached eggs like a dog tearing a steak, chomping them with the grandest vigor.

"Yum!" she said, taking a bite of shortbread and then scooping up a forkful of mash in the same mouthful.

Rupert carefully cut his omelet. He took a few bites, and slid the book back over to him. He opened back to the same page and reread. "Hmm. I'm not sure what this means, but if we pull it apart word by word, I'm sure we can figure it out."

Witchling Two scratched her head in response. "You can do it, Rupert! You're the smartest apprentice I've ever had."

"But I'm the *only* apprentice you've ever had."

"Which means you're also the best apprentice I've ever had."

"Okay, I'll help!" Rupert said, grinning. "But let's start at page one. The first problem is we're trying to start in the middle instead of the beginning."

"Yes, yes, very smart!" Witchling Two said, gnawing on a biscuit.

He flipped the book back to the Introduction section.

"Uh-oh," said Witchling Two. She hid behind her book and pointed toward the cash register, where two strange figures were standing. There was a very tall, knobbly looking woman with the blackest of black eyes, rigidly pointy eyebrows, and long black hair in a braid. She had a tight face—one that pulled her skin in all directions, as if she'd weathered centuries of time.

The second witch was much younger. Rupert thought she looked just a bit younger than his mother—she had no wrinkles at all. Just narrow eyes, a slight smile, and a hook nose. Her hair was also black, but it was loose and wild.

They caught his eye, and Rupert's stomach turned over like a roasting pig on a spit.

"Act natural," Witchling Two whispered. She began to whistle loudly, which turned into a hum, which turned into a song that she chanted loudly while banging her spoon and fork on her ceramic plate:

LA DE DA DE DA DE DA.

NOTHING TO SEE HERE

NOTHING AT ALL

PLEASE MOVE ALONG

FEEL FREE TO DISAPPEAR!

Act natural? Rupert rolled his eyes. This was about as unnatural as anyone could possibly get.

He wasn't surprised at all when the two women came over to their table. As they approached, one of the tea shop's patrons squeaked in fear, frantically packed her belongings, and left the shop. The older woman leered as the woman left, as though she was taking delight in her panicked flight. Everybody else in the tea shop seemed unconcerned.

"Well, well, well," said the younger woman. "So the rumors *are* true."

"What rumors?" Witchling Two said.

"You've teamed up with a *human*."

The older woman clapped her hands together. "Oh!" she crowed. "This is going to be good!"

Rupert's heart leaped. These ladies certainly

looked and sounded like witches, but if they were . . . well, then, he was cooked. He was positively dead in the water. He could only imagine what horrible punishment they would inflict upon him. He desperately looked for an exit, but they were blocking his only way out of the booth. He stared up into their faces. Which witches were they? Certainly not the dreaded Fairfoul Witch, right? He gulped and wiped his sweaty palms on his pants.

"Who—who are you?"

"Brave little one, aren't we?" the older woman said with a twisted grin.

Rupert could feel the sweat droplets forming on the back of his neck. He positively quaked with fear.

"How did you find us?" Witchling Two said. She looked almost too calm.

"We followed you here," said the younger woman. "If you're going to gallivant with humans, you shouldn't be so obvious about it."

"*Honestly,*" said the older one, sounding cross. "Studying spells in a dingy old tea shop that's on the same alley as our shops? You might as well have worn a target on your chest."

Witchling Two blushed. "I-I wasn't thinking—

you're right, this was terribly stupid of me. I j-just thought that since the Fairfoul Witch always sleeps during the day and the Midnight Witch is at Foxbury this weekend . . . But still! I'm sorry, Rupert. I didn't mean to put you in danger again." She looked at Rupert, ashamed.

He opened his mouth, but no words came out. The two women were glaring at him with their stony, black, bulging eyes. All of his insides were cold.

"Rupert?" said Witchling Two. "Are you all right? You're looking . . . ill."

"They're w-w-witches!" he sputtered.

The two women threw their heads back and cackled. They held onto each other and laughed for a good long time, and just when Rupert thought they were done laughing, they looked at one another and cracked up again. He could feel his cheeks flush.

"Ah, you found a smarty-pants," the younger woman said, dabbing at her eyes with her sleeves.

Witchling Two patted his arm. "Rupert, don't worry. These are my guardians. This is the Nebulous Witch. But I just call her Nebby." She pointed to the younger witch with the beak nose and wild black hair. "And this is the Storm Witch. I call her, well, Storm," she said, gesturing toward the old, wrinkly, pointy-eyebrowed one. "You're safe with them—"

"Don't let the boy get too comfortable with us," Nebby said coldly. "We are *not* pleased."

"How dare you disgrace the name of the witch?" Storm howled. "You're coming home right now. How can you muck around with your Bar Exam just around the corner?"

"I'm not mucking around, Storm," Witchling Two said. "This boy is helping me practice my magic."

"Well, I'll say!" Storm said. Her pointy eyebrows shot so far up that Rupert was afraid they would recede into her hairline. "In my day, we *never* conversed with humanlings."

"He's called boy," Witchling Two said.

"Actually, he's called Rupert," Rupert said, but then he cupped a hand over his mouth.

"Move over," Nebby said, eyeing Rupert with distaste.

Rupert scooted to the end of the booth as fast as he could, and Nebby sat down next to him. Storm scooched next to Witchling Two.

Nebby frowned. "Now tell us, Witchling Two, what in the world do you think you're doing?"

"Please—Storm. Nebby," Witchling Two said. "You two have your Witches Council business, and I need someone to help me. If you don't want me bothering you, then I need Rupert."

Nebby shook her head. "This is, without a doubt, the worst idea you've ever had."

"But I want to keep him. Please? Pretty please? Pretty please with lollipops on top?"

Storm snorted. "He's not a pet, Witchling! You can't keep him! And more importantly, we can't guarantee protection from the other witches—for either of you. This is *madness*."

Rupert cleared his throat, and they all turned toward him. "Well, if you ask me, I really would like to help Witchling Two with her Bar Exam."

"Oh *really*?" Storm said. "You'd like to help? Do you know anything about magic? Spell casting, brewing, witch laws, witch customs?"

"Not exactly, but—"

"It's settled," Nebby said calmly, putting up her hand for silence. "Witchling Two, you'll come back home and study for your exam in your room. Boy, you'll forget all about this."

"No!" Witchling Two and Rupert said together.

Nebby shook her head. "Witchling, you're endangering yourself, this boy, and Storm and me, too. If the Fairfoul Witch finds out about this, she'll have *all* our heads, not just yours."

"Poo," Witchling Two said with a pout. "I don't want you to get in trouble. But what about Rupert? He's my new friend!"

"If you were really a friend to him, you'd end this relationship right now."

"But what if I do a better job at keeping him a secret? Then I can have my apprentice, you won't get in trouble, and he won't need to be protected—"

"I forbid this," Nebby said firmly. "Don't make us use magic to make you separate," she threatened.

Witchling Two glared at her guardians. But then her glare melted away. She sighed, folded her arms, and leaned back against the booth. "Oh, all right,"

Witchling Two said with a casual shrug. "I suppose this was a stupid idea anyway. I mean, what does this *boy* know about magic?"

"Hey!" Rupert said. "I thought you said I was the smartest apprentice you ever had!"

Witchling Two wouldn't meet his gaze.

Storm stood with a flourish of her black robes. "I say! What are we waiting for? Let's go!"

Seriously? After all that, he wasn't going to be a witch's apprentice after all? "But wait—"

"Good riddance!" Nebby said.

"Harrumph!" Storm said.

"Good-bye forever!" Witchling Two said.

Storm pulled Witchling Two out of the tea shop by the hand, and Rupert watched helplessly as his only friend marched out of his life for good.

Vocabulary Class

AFTER THE STRANGEST, MOST WONDERFUL, AND most heartbreaking long weekend as a witch's apprentice, Rupert did not want to return to his old life in Mrs. Frabbleknacker's class for one minute. But he took his seat next to Kyle Mason-Reed and Allison Gormley. They both looked straight ahead with wide eyes. Rupert sighed and did the same.

Moments later, Mrs. Frabbleknacker clip-clopped into the room, and Rupert caught the whiff of belly-button lint again. He bit on his lips to keep from making a sour face. The last time he had made a sour face in Mrs. Frabbleknacker's class, she made him keep ten marbles in his mouth for an hour. And when Rupert spit them out, to his horror, there were only nine.

Mrs. Frabbleknacker tapped on the board with her long fingernails. The whole class tensed. They were waiting for her to scratch the board, for her fingernails to make that high-pitched, shudder-inducing moan, but Mrs. Frabbleknacker peeled away from the board.

"Children," she said, as though she was saying something truly awful like *Root Canal* or *Pickled Sausages.* "Today we will study vocabulary."

She turned around and quickly wrote four words on the board:

REPUGNANT

TACITURN

CLAMOR

ABSCOND

Rupert's jaw dropped.

"Those aren't words!" Bruno Gopp called out. "Those are just funny sounds put together!"

Mrs. Frabbleknacker's head twisted around the back of her shoulder. Her eyes were wide and wild. "Did you speak without raising your hand?"

Bruno Gopp cowered. "N-no, ma'am," he whispered. "I didn't say anything—it wasn't me."

Mrs. Frabbleknacker took a step closer to Bruno, and Rupert was sure that his friend was about to wet himself. Sweat dripped down Bruno's forehead, and every kid in the class held his breath.

Mrs. Frabbleknacker sucked air through her crooked nose. "And are you *lying* to me—again?"

Bruno looked around, as if he hoped that someone in the class would feed him the correct answer. "No?"

Mrs. Frabbleknacker lunged forward and grabbed Bruno by the ear. Bruno winced in pain, muttering *ow, ow, ow, ow!* She pulled him to the front of the class and threw him into a wooden chair. Bruno trembled as Mrs. Frabbleknacker placed a box of toothpicks in front of him.

"P-please don't stab me with those," Bruno said.

Mrs. Frabbleknacker leaned forward and breathed into the ear she almost pulled off. "You won't leave this classroom until you build a tower. Just one toothpick on top of the other. Longways. Use them all."

"But that's impossible," Bruno said. "Not without glue."

"I hope you said good-bye to your family this morning," Mrs. Frabbleknacker said, and then she burst into a deep, hearty laugh.

When Mrs. Frabbleknacker finished laughing, she snapped back to the rest of the class. "Well? You've had ten minutes to learn the words. Now it's time for a test."

The entire class gasped.

"Allison!" Mrs. Frabbleknacker snapped. She walked up to Allison's desk and breathed her banana breath in Allison's nervous-looking face. "What is REPUGNANT?"

"Um," Allison stammered. "Is it a kind of dog?"

Mrs. Frabbleknacker flipped Allison's desk over and tossed her papers across the room. "NO!" she shouted. "IT'S YOU! *YOU* ARE REPUGNANT, YOU LOATHESOME CHILD! YOU ARE THE UGLIEST, SMELLIEST, ROTTEN-BEYOND-ROTTEN LITTLE GIRL IN THE WHOLE WORLD!"

Allison ran from the classroom crying.

"Next," Mrs. Frabbleknacker said. "Francis. Demonstrate TACITURN!"

Francis was too afraid to move, blink, or even breathe. He sat there in silence.

Mrs. Frabbleknacker frowned, clearly disappointed. "Correct. Now class, demonstrate TACITURN."

Every student imitated Francis—his straight posture, his nauseated expression, his still and silent demeanor, and even his tiny eye twitch. And without knowing what TACITURN was, the whole class became it.

"Kaleigh—CLAMOR."

"Oh! My daddy had mussels and CLAMORS for dinner last night!"

Mrs. Frabbleknacker smiled wickedly. "Did I not ask the class to be TACITURN? Did I ever say to *stop* being TACITURN?"

"Wh-what's TACITURN?"

"SILENCE!" Mrs. Frabbleknacker shouted. "SILENCE, SILENCE, SILENCE! AND WHEN YOU SPEAK, ARE YOU SILENT?" Mrs. Frabbleknacker licked her lips, her long tongue fluttering in and out of her mouth like a snake. "ARE YOU TACITURN, KALEIGH?"

"No, but you asked me a question."

"TACITURN! TACITURN, TACITURN! AND YOUR FATHER DID *NOT* HAVE CLAMORS FOR DINNER BECAUSE I AM CLAMORING NOW. DO YOU HEAR WHAT I AM DOING?"

Kaleigh nodded taciturnly.

The whole room buzzed with silence. Then, Rupert heard the sound of a hundred toothpicks falling against a table. *Poor Bruno,* he thought.

"And now that I have you all silent," Mrs. Frabbleknacker said, "I will demonstrate the last vocabulary word, ABSCOND."

Mrs. Frabbleknacker walked out of the classroom, slamming the door in her wake.

Two hours later, Rupert and his classmates decided it was finally safe to move. Mrs. Frabbleknacker wasn't coming back.

New Lair, Where?

WHEN RUPERT ARRIVED AT HIS HOUSE, WITCHLING Two was waiting for him on the porch.

She waved to him, grinning. "Hi, Rupert!"

He was almost too stunned for words. Finally he stammered out, "What are *you* doing here?"

"I came to see my apprentice! What are *you* doing here?"

"I live here."

"Well, there we have it," she said with a nod.

Rupert climbed the porch steps, but as he got closer, the smile slid off her freckly face. She wiggled her nose and sniffed loudly. "You smell funny," she said.

"Do I smell like bananas? Mrs. Frabbleknacker may have rubbed off on me."

"No, you smell more like pigeon liver," she said matter-of-factly.

"What are you doing here?" Rupert said. "You said I didn't know anything about magic."

"It's called perverse apology. Nebby and Storm use it on me all the time, so I thought I'd trick them for once."

Rupert scratched his head. "Perverse apology? I think you mean *reverse psychology*."

Witchling Two shrugged.

"So what are you doing *here*? At my house? My mom doesn't particularly like . . . people like you. You better leave before she gets home from work."

"I've already met Joanne. We just had a nice pot of tea."

At that moment, Rupert's mother opened the front door. She was struggling to get her shoes on, and she was wiggling around trying to clip the straps. "Rupert, honey, you didn't tell me you made such a lovely friend at school. We were just having tea."

Rupert looked at Witchling Two in fright, but she was just smiling. Did she tell his mother the truth? Rupert couldn't imagine that Witchling Two would tell his mother that she was a witch and Rupert was her new apprentice—and his mother seemed far too calm to have heard that she was just drinking tea with a witch.

"Rupert?" his mother said. "You seem distracted."

"Sorry. You've met my friend . . ." he tried to introduce her, but then he realized that he very well couldn't introduce her as Witchling Two. "Uh, my friend. So now we're going to work on homework. In my room." Rupert grabbed the sleeve of Witchling Two's powder blue shirt, and he pulled her into the house.

"I'm headed to work!" his mother shouted behind him. "I'll see you later, Rupert!"

"Nice to meet you, Mrs. Campbell!" Witchling Two cried.

Rupert pulled her past the kitchen and through the living room. He tried to drag her up the stairs, but she paused at the adjacent basement door.

"Ooooh!" she squealed. "A dark and dangerous door! What's in there?"

"Just the basement," he said. "Let's not go down there."

Witchling Two opened the basement door, grabbed

Rupert's arm, and pulled him down the stairs with her. The basement wasn't the most comfortable part of the house—it was a carpet-less, cement-floored, dimly lit, dust-ridden, musty-smelling, dingy old space. But despite his reluctance to go down there, Rupert supposed it was perfect for what he needed at the moment: a quiet area to think. He buried his face in his hands and thought, thought, thought about what to do next. Now that his mother met Witchling Two, it changed everything. His mom would expect to see his "new friend" around. But how could Rupert possibly have her over? She was a *witch*, and if his mother found out, she wouldn't like that one bit.

Rupert looked up to find Witchling Two pacing the perimeter of the room.

"What are you doing?" Rupert said.

"The dimensions are perfect. And it's just the right temperature. And it has the ideal amount of light."

"For . . . for what?"

"For my new lair, of course!"

Rupert's stomach dropped. *"What?"*

"Well, I can't go back to Pexale Close with you.

The Witches Council booby-trapped it for humans."

"You can't have a lair here!" Rupert said. "My mom hates witches! And she'll know if a witch's lair is in her own basement!"

"Calm down, Rupert. She likes me."

"Not when she finds out you're a witch! And what did you tell her by the way? How did you end up having tea with my mom?"

Witchling Two smiled. "Ah, well, I was waiting for you outside the house, and your mom just invited me in. Who am I to say no to perfectly good tea and crumpets?"

"And what did you say when she asked for your name?"

"I didn't say anything. I just changed the subject."

"Do you know what name you'll want to use, eventually?"

Witchling Two shook her head. "Not yet. I'll keep you posted. But you have to promise to keep it a secret. I'll be very upset if one of the other witch-lings takes my name."

Witchling Two turned her back toward Rupert and put her arms straight in the air. Then she stretched from left to right. Then right to left. Then she jumped up in the air. Then she jumped up in the air and waved her arms. Then she crouched down on the ground. Then she hugged her knees. Then she put her cheek to the floor. Then the other one. Then she stood on her head until her face turned purple.

"Are you all right?" Rupert said.

"I have to do my exercises now. Shhh," she said.

Rupert sat on the worktable and observed Witchling Two's routine with bemusement. "You're looking rather purple."

"That's my favorite color!"

"So I've heard," Rupert said, "but it might be healthier if you stayed peach."

Witchling Two flipped up to her feet. "Let's do some magic!"

Rupert's eyes bulged, which was his way of saying *NO WAY, JOSE*. They could not—absolutely, positively, definitely, surely, certainly could NOT—use his basement as a lair. Because even though his mother worked three jobs, she was bound to notice a cauldron in the basement.

Witchling Two cracked her knuckles, and Rupert cringed. He hated the sound, and it just so happens that witches have extra crackily knuckles that make the whole room shake. It was the loudest, most horrible sound Rupert had heard in all eleven years of his life.

"AUGH!"

And Witchling Two froze. "What is it?" she whispered. "Did you see . . . a bunny rabbit?"

And then everything clicked for Rupert.

"Oh yes!" Rupert lied. "I saw a bunny! There are tons of them in the basement. *Millions,* in fact. All the bunnies in the world live in basements. Maybe you don't want your lair here after all—"

Witchling Two jumped onto the table. "BUUUUNNNNNYYYYYYYYYYYYYYYY! AAAAAAAAHHHHHHHHHHHHHHHHHHHHH-HHHHH!"

"NO NO!" Rupert said. "I WAS JUST KIDDING!"

But then Witchling Two whimpered. And that whimper turned into a snivel. And that snivel turned into a weep. And that weep turned into a cry. And that cry turned into a wail. And that wail turned into a sob. And that sob turned into a blubber.

And by that time, the basement began to flood.

Hic!

RUPERT JUMPED OFF THE TABLE, AND WITCHLING Two's tear-water sloshed into the mesh of his sneakers. Her tears were already at Rupert's ankles. He slopped and splattered and splashed toward the closet under the staircase. Rupert yanked on the door handle, and the door very reluctantly opened against the current of tear-water.

Rupert dug around in the dark, dank closet and came out holding a bucket. He scooped some of Witchling Two's tear-water into the bucket, ran upstairs, and dumped it in the sink. Then he ran back and did it again.

"Please," he said, after Witchling Two stopped howling so loudly, "don't cry! I was only teasing.

There are no bunnies. They don't exist in Gliver-stoll, and certainly not in my basement."

Witchling Two hiccupped, tears still flowing.

"You're flooding my basement . . . and your lair."

Witchling Two hiccupped again. *Hic!*

Rupert couldn't believe what he was about to say, but he knew that it might be the only way to get Witchling Two to stop flooding his house. "That's right," Rupert said. "If you stop crying, I'll let you use my basement as a lair. Promise."

"But I *hic!* don't know *hic!* if I can stop. *Hic!*"

"You have to," Rupert said. "Or else you'll flood my entire house. And then my mom will find out. And then I won't be allowed to be your apprentice anymore. And you might not pass your Bar Exam. And then you'll never get a name."

Hic!

"Be right back!" Rupert said as he ran upstairs to dump out another bucket of water.

Rupert hopped up the stairs, accidentally slosh-ing water on the carpet of the first-floor hallway. He carefully speed-walked the rest of the way to the sink and dumped the water out again.

He ran back to the basement, his sneakers making SQUISHY noises and leaking water everywhere. The tear-water was up to Rupert's thighs now, and he tried not to think about what he would do if the water rose any higher.

Witchling Two still cradled her knees and hiccupped on the worktable. She dipped her bare toe into the water, and then curled up again. "Ru*hic!*pert," she sputtered. "My *hic!* cauldron." Witchling Two reached into her pocket and pulled out a flat piece of plastic. "It's my *hic!* por*hic!*able, inflatable cauldron! *Hic!*"

Rupert tore the cauldron away from her and blew into the plastic mouthpiece. The more he blew, the bigger the cauldron became—until it became so big that Rupert could fit inside the middle. Rupert tried to pass it off to Witchling Two, but she shook her head and backed away from it.

"No!" she said. "If I *hic!* touch it, it will *hic!* turn to iron!"

Rupert looked at it in confusion. "Well, what do I do with it?"

"Set it *hic!* in the water." Witchling Two held her hands over the floating plastic cauldron and snapped her fingers. "Get this water *hic!* up, and drain it until the basement's neat," she said.

The cauldron whizzed and whirred, and the tear-water in the basement began to churn. Then the whirling and twirling and swirling got faster and faster. Rupert jumped onto the table just in time— and then the cauldron sucked all the water into its middle like a vacuum.

For a minute, Rupert and Witchling Two held onto each other, listening only to Witchling Two's occasional *hic!*s. Then Rupert climbed off the table and peered into the cauldron. There was nothing inside. He examined the floor and the legs of the table, and they were both dry. Even his sneakers were dry.

Witchling Two crawled off the table, too, beaming. "Did I . . . actually perform a spell correctly?" she said, suppressing a hiccup.

"I think so—"

POP!

The cauldron exploded—smoke, light, dust, and all of the tear-water burst out. The water fell on their heads in fat droplets like a heavy rain. Then all of the sudden, the water turned into freezing ice pellets that plunked them in the head. Rupert pulled Witchling Two under the table to avoid getting hit.

"THE CAULDRON WASN'T BIG ENOUGH!" shouted Rupert.

"YES IT WAS!" shouted Witchling Two.

"THEN IT WAS YOUR SPELL!"

"MAYBE!"

Rupert tried to recall what she had said—and realized with horror. "GET THIS WATER *HIC!* UP AND DRAIN UNTIL THE BASEMENT'S NEAT," he recited.

"WHAT?"

"THAT'S WHAT YOU SAID!" Rupert told her.

"WHAT'S WHAT I SAID?"

"YOU SAID GET THIS WATER *HIC!* UP AND DRAIN UNTIL THE BASEMENT'S NEAT, BUT YOUR SPELL MESSED UP. IT'S GETTING THIS WATER *PICKED* UP AND *RAINING* UNTIL THE BASEMENT *SLEETS!*"

Witchling Two put a hand to her mouth, then sank into her own icy tear-water in shame. "I'll never pass my Bar Exam!" she bubbled into the water, and then she started to whimper. And that whimper turned into a snivel. And that snivel turned into a weep. And that weep turned into nothing because Rupert ran over and shook her by the shoulders.

"No crying!" he said. "From now on, you can only cry when you're happy . . . like humans."

Witchling Two nodded.

Rupert handed her a bucket, retrieved a mop from the closet, and the two of them set off on a long afternoon of very arduous manual labor.

There's Such a Thing as Too Friendly

RUPERT HAD TO ADMIT—HE REALLY LIKED BEING a witchling's apprentice. Now that they were all hidden from the Witches Council and the basement was no longer flooded with tears, Rupert felt better about his new job and his new friend.

For the past few days, they had spent each day after school preparing Rupert's basement to be Witchling Two's new lair. In the dead of night, Witchling Two had trudged back to her old lair and dragged her state-of-the-art copper cauldron and a few jars of unusual ingredients to Rupert's house. Rupert had felt guilty that she had to do it alone, but her lair was still human booby-trapped.

Besides, Witchling Two was really sneaky about getting her items out of her lair and into Rupert's house. She did it while the Witches Council was in session, and then she hid in a tree until Rupert's mother had left for work. After Rupert's mother was gone, Rupert had no qualms about helping Witchling Two lug her stuff inside.

He made Witchling Two set up her lair in the back corner of the room, so that his mother couldn't immediately see it from the top of the steps. Plus, he didn't think his mother had been in the basement for years. The thick cobwebs were proof of that. With her three jobs, she was just too busy to do anything except collapse when she got home from work.

Rupert had put Witchling Two's ingredients on bookshelves covered with old drapes full of mothballs, and he hid the cauldron underneath a tarpaulin. Then, they devised a sneaking system, so that Witchling Two could get in and out of her lair without being caught. This involved Rupert unlatching the basement window, which was just large enough for Witchling Two.

The system was working great so far, and Rupert's mom didn't suspect a thing. Everything was working perfectly—except for Witchling Two's magic. With all the hustle and bustle of getting her lair organized, unfortunately, they didn't have any time to practice. She only had three weeks left until her Bar Exam, and she was just as terrible as ever.

Witchling Two chattered constantly about the potions they would brew and the spells they would cast, but much to Rupert's disappointment, he and Witchling Two still hadn't actually practiced any magic. Witchling Two claimed they needed some more fresh ingredients for her potions, but Rupert had the sneaking suspicion that she was trying to avoid practicing the subjects she didn't like.

On Saturday, Rupert dragged Witchling Two to the grocery store to get the ingredients she needed.

"What do we need to buy?" Rupert asked Witchling Two as she skipped around the fresh produce.

Witchling Two paused and thought. "We need some rhubarb, parsley, chicken bones, and lollipops."

Rupert stopped walking. "Lollipops?" he said. "For the potions?"

"Well, sure . . . if we need some loll or pop in a potion we could always just put one in."

Rupert was not convinced. "So, the lollipops aren't for the potions, then."

Witchling Two smacked her lips. Rupert thought he detected a bit of drool at the corner of her mouth.

"You are an addict," he said, "and you have a problem."

Witchling Two grinned and kept skipping.

"When are we going to get back to practicing your magic?" Rupert asked. "Don't you need to pass your Bar Exam?"

The witchling turned a sickly shade of gray. "Well, strictly speaking, technically, theoretically, notionally, supposedly, hypothetically, in principle, maybe, perhaps, possibly, yes," she stammered.

"What happens if you don't pass your Bar Exam?"

Witchling Two stopped in front of the cauliflower, her eyes wide and terrified. "Expulsion," she whispered. "Exile. Shame. They strip me of my powers, and then I'm forced to leave my family and wander nomadically, never to return home again."

"And I thought being grounded was bad."

"Not passing the Bar Exam is the worst thing that can ever happen to a witch."

"So why aren't we working on your spells?"

"More ingredients, Rupert. More, more, more. We can't brew a proper potion without more ingredients."

"But I thought you were worse at spells than potions—"

"MORE INGREDIENTS! MORE, MORE, MORE," she shouted, plugging her ears.

Rupert laughed and slipped his hands in his pockets.

He followed Witchling Two as she inspected vegetables with one eye open. Occasionally, she would sniff an item, and very rarely she took a nibble. Whenever she did nibble on something, she put it back on the shelves.

Rupert cringed. No wonder his mother always insisted on microwavable food.

When they got to the sweets and candies aisle, Rupert saw Kyle shopping with his father. Rupert and Kyle looked at each other and froze. Then Rupert backed out of the aisle, dragging Witchling Two by the arm.

"We don't need candy," Rupert said. "Let's just go—please."

Witchling Two looked behind her, then back at Rupert, trying to understand what just happened.

"Who was that boy?" Witchling Two said. "Is he trouble? A bully? Do I need to teach him a lesson?" she said, cracking her knuckles.

Rupert shuddered from the sound. "No!" he said. "It's just a boy in my class . . . we used to be friends . . ."

"What, what?" Witchling Two begged, her eyes growing wide. "What happened?"

"Mrs. Frabbleknacker," Rupert said. "She won't let any of us be friends anymore. We're not allowed to talk to each other in class or outside of class— hey, wait!" Rupert said as Witchling Two marched toward the candy aisle. "Wait—no! What are you doing? No! Stop it—no!"

Rupert ran to the candy aisle, but it was too late—Witchling Two was already at the end of the aisle, next to Kyle and his dad. She stuck out a hand and smiled brightly. "Hello!" she said. "What's your name?"

Kyle looked like he was going to explode. He looked at Rupert for help, but Rupert looked down. He couldn't be caught talking to Kyle, and if Kyle knew what was best for him, he'd ignore Witchling Two as well.

"Er . . . I'm Kyle Mason-Reed."

"Kyle Mason-Reed, huh? I think I've seen you at school. Well, Rupert and I were wondering if you'd like to come to the movies with us next weekend." Witchling Two smiled at Kyle's father and batted her eyes innocently. "Would that be okay Mr. Mason-Reed?" she asked Kyle's father.

"It's just Mr. Mason," Kyle's father said. "And Kyle is at his mother's house next weekend—but it should be okay with her. It's certainly okay with me." Kyle's father rolled the shopping cart out of the candy aisle and called for Kyle to meet him after he exchanged numbers with the nice girl.

Kyle grabbed Witchling Two on the arm. "I am *not* going to the movies with you and Rupert."

"Why not?"

"Because I want to stay alive." Kyle looked around the supermarket and lowered his voice to the faintest whisper. "You must be from Miss Snugglybuns's class, so you probably don't understand. But I'm in Mrs. Frabbleknacker's class, which means that I can't talk to Rupert. She'll know. I shouldn't even be talking to *you*!"

"That's nonsense," Witchling Two said. "You guys

are friends—you can't let Mrs. Frabbleknacker stop you from talking."

Kyle dropped her arm and scurried down the candy aisle. He stopped when he was near Rupert, but neither boy looked at the other.

"Rupert," said Kyle, to a bag of milk chocolate bars. "Are you insane? You think Bruno's toothpick punishment was bad? If Mrs. Frabbleknacker finds out that you've made friends with someone in Miss Snugglybuns's class, she'll probably make you swallow all those toothpicks whole!"

"Maybe," said Rupert, suddenly feeling brave and daring. He peeled his eyes away from the shortbread cookies and looked directly at Kyle. "You're probably right . . . and maybe I'll get stomach splinters, but it's a whole lot better than not having any friends."

Rupert marched to where Witchling Two was beaming with pride. He wheeled the cartful of potion ingredients to the cashier and paid with the emergency money his mother gave him. Then, he grabbed the bags of groceries and headed out of the store with Witchling Two in tow.

As they walked home, Rupert hoped he wouldn't regret talking to Kyle. He had disobeyed Mrs. Frabbleknacker's orders. And was what he said to Kyle even true? Was having friends really worth swallowing toothpicks?

Rupert hugged the paper grocery bag to his chest as he listened to Witchling Two chatter on and on about how right Rupert was.

What?

WHEN RUPERT AND WITCHLING TWO ARRIVED at Rupert's house with their groceries, they sorted them into different shelves. Witchling Two gleefully chattered about the health benefits of lollipops, but Rupert hardly even listened.

Sometimes a very good mood can turn very sour in a matter of minutes, and that's exactly how Rupert felt. His stomach twisted, his palms sticky, his mouth dry—Rupert knew he had made a mistake. He definitely, positively, without a doubt should not have talked to Kyle. And he shouldn't be talking to Witchling Two, either, because a horde of witches, not to mention his mother, would disapprove. It was the wrong thing to do.

"Rupert?" Witchling Two said. "What do you think?"

"Huh? Think about what?"

Witchling Two sighed a long exaggerated sigh. "Cherry-flavored lollipops versus watermelon!"

Rupert rolled his eyes.

Witchling Two nodded vigorously. "That's exactly how I feel. They are *both* subpar to grape."

Rupert scrunched his face real tight in anticipation of what he knew he had to say. "Witchling Two," he said, "would you mind going home for the night?"

"Go home?" Witchling Two said meekly, her voice soft and hushed.

Rupert cringed for fear that she would burst into tears again.

"Why, that's a splendid idea!" she shouted, leaping to her feet.

"It is?" Rupert said, sounding less convinced.

"Of course! You want me to go home and take a written exam, right? Oh, Rupert! You are such a wonderful apprentice—you keep me on task!"

"Y-yes," Rupert said. "Perhaps you should take a written exam."

"Right! Because we need to let the ingredients rot

a bit before we can use them, and goodness knows I'm rubbish at spells, so the only thing left for me to practice is the WHATs."

"What?"

"WHATs!"

"What's what?"

"What's WHATs?"

Rupert scratched his head. "I'm confused," he said. "What are we talking about?"

"The WHATs—the Witchling Handwritten Aptitude Test! It's part of my examination. I need to pass the written WHATs and the two practical tests: brewing and spell casting. And you're right, Rupert . . . I've been focusing too much on brewing and spell casting."

"I said that?"

Witchling Two nodded.

Rupert escorted her to the basement window to see her off.

Witchling Two turned to Rupert, an expression of resolve on her face. "Cheers, Rupert!" she said. "I'm off to . . . what's that human expression? I'm off to kiss the crooks!"

"Hit the books," corrected Rupert.

"Yes, assist the cooks," Witchling Two said as she made her way to the window. "See you tomorrow, Rupert!" And then she slipped into the darkness and was gone.

Rupert closed the window, walked upstairs, and sat at the kitchen table. He read *The Unabridged History of the Oxford Comma*—a book that Mrs. Frabbleknacker had assigned his class—until he heard the front door open and shut again. His mother came in, carrying an enormous tub of ice cream.

"Mom!" Rupert said, rushing to give her a hug.

"My, my! If only I got this type of greeting every time I came home from work!"

"Sorry . . . I've been busy," Rupert said.

His mother sniffed, and Rupert knew what was coming next. Sometimes he felt like his mother had extrasensory powers and was instantly able to tell whenever Rupert was sad about something. His mother plopped the ice cream on the counter. "What is it?" she said. "What's wrong? Wait! Hold that thought!" His mother ran into the pantry and grabbed two bowls and two spoons and scooped out two enormous helpings of Mr. and Mrs. Gummyum's new flavor: carrot ice cream.

She set the bowls on the table and sat next to Rupert.

"What's going on, Rupert?"

Rupert took a deep breath. He twiddled his spoon between his fingers. "Do you think . . . am I a bad kid?"

"That depends," his mother teased. "What did you do?"

"Nothing," Rupert said, taking a big spoonful of ice cream. "Hmm. So this is what a vegetable tastes like?"

"Funny."

"Carrot flavor . . . not bad."

"I agree," his mother said, wiping her lips with a napkin.

Rupert sighed. "Mom, I have this friend. But sometimes I feel like we shouldn't be friends because—"

"Oh, Rupert, I loved your little friend. What was her name again?"

"Mooooom," Rupert whined.

"I'm sorry . . . finish your story."

"Anyway, there are a lot of people who think we shouldn't be friends," Rupert said, thinking of Mrs. Frabbleknacker, the Witches Council, Nebby,

Storm, and his mother. "But I like her. She's a good friend, and she makes me happy. . . ."

"There's your answer, Rupert," his mother said. "If you like her, that's all that really matters. No one else has the right to tell you who you can or cannot be friends with." His mother paused. "That would be a great fortune cookie—let me write that down." She grabbed a small notebook and a pen from her purse and scribbled it down.

"Are you even listening to me, Mom?" Rupert asked.

"Hold on . . . *can or cannot be friends with,*" his mother recited. "Okay. Sorry."

Rupert drummed his fingers on the table. "Mom, what if an adult told me not to be friends with her?"

"Adult, kid, squirrel—it doesn't matter, Rupert. You just be friends with whoever treats you well and makes you happy, and that's all you can do."

Rupert smiled. His mother always knew exactly what to say to make him feel better.

Once Upon a Time in Gliverstoll

Every day for the next four days, Rupert invited Witchling Two over. And thanks to the talk with his mom, he didn't even feel guilty about it.

But on Thursday night, she decided to practice the WHATs by herself, which worked out well because Rupert needed to make a poster about the history of processed potatoes for Mrs. Frabbleknacker's class. Rupert was working on the assignment in his room when he heard a tapping noise at his window. He turned around to see Witchling Two bobbing up and down outside on a broomstick.

"PSSSST!" she shouted. "LET ME IN! BUT BE QUIET!"

Rupert ran to the window and opened it enough so that Witchling Two could fly into his room and crash-land on his bed.

"What are you doing here?" Rupert said. "I thought you were studying for the WHATs again tonight!"

"I was," Witchling Two said. "But I got bored."

"You only have two weeks until your exam!"

"So?"

"So you can't just stop doing your homework when you get bored," Rupert said. "You'll never get an A that way."

"An A? What's that?"

"Never mind," Rupert said. "So what are you here for? Want to brew something?"

Witchling Two nodded. "Yes, and I have the perfect concoction!"

Rupert followed Witchling Two as she skipped down the steps and walked into the kitchen. She put up a pot of water and turned the stove on high.

"You need boiling water for this potion?"

Witchling Two nodded with her tongue sticking out. She giggled and sniggered into her hands. Then she threw her head back and cackled. "I'm brewing . . . HOT CHOCOLATE!" she said.

Rupert was used to her odd antics by now, so he just shrugged his shoulders.

"Can I ask you a question about witches?" Rupert said, when Witchling Two had calmed down.

"I don't know if I'm allowed to answer, but you can certainly ask."

"Were they always in Gliverstoll? How did they get here? And what do they do?"

The water began to bubble, and Witchling Two retrieved two mugs from the cabinet. She dumped the chocolate powder into the mugs and then poured the water. She added whipped cream on top for a little touch of flair, and then she handed Rupert a mug.

"Let me tell you a story," Witchling Two said, sitting down at the kitchen table. She took a sip of her hot chocolate, and the whipped cream formed a white mustache on her lip. "The story is called: *The History of Gliverstoll.* Are you ready for it?"

Rupert nodded and sipped his hot chocolate.

"Once upon a time there was a rocky hill by an ocean. This place is what would eventually be known as the town of Higgenwatsenstinkybottom—before the town council overrode this name and changed it to Gliverstoll. Anyway, this town was infected."

"Infected?" Rupert said. "With what?"

"With *bunnies!*" she whispered, with a spooky edge to her voice. She wiggled her fingers for added effect.

"Are you sure this is historically accurate?"

"Positive," Witchling Two said.

"But where did the witches come from?"

"The ancient witches were nomads, flying around on their tree branches (brooms weren't invented yet). They stopped wherever and whenever they had a good reason to stop. As they were flying over Gliverstoll, they felt the land call out to them, almost like the town was drawing them in. After feeling this magnetic pull, the witches decided to take a closer look, and that's when they saw a gazillion bunnies hopping around, looking all fluffy and evil. Well, they couldn't just fly by and leave the poor townspeople at the mercy of these devilish creatures. So the witches stopped and banished the bunnies.

"Anyway, the townspeople of Higgenwatsenstinkybottom were so grateful to the witches that they offered to share their home. And the witches loved the town of Higgenwatsenstinkybottom so much that they agreed. They stopped their wandering and decided to stay here, where they felt like they belonged."

"And how long ago was this?" Rupert asked. "In human years, not witch years please."

Witchling Two scratched her head. "Well if my conversion scale is correct, then this was hundreds of thousands of millions of billions of years ago, and this has been our home ever since."

"Hmm," Rupert said. "But what do you guys do?"

"I'm not allowed to tell you," Witchling Two said. "Even though you're my apprentice, I still have to keep witch secrets. Just know that you're in good hands." Witchling Two looked around frantically, leaned close to Rupert, and whispered, "We keep the climate favorable, we circulate commerce, and we bring tourists in on our brooms. The more money the townspeople make, the more we make, too. And the more money we make, the more potions we can concoct. And the more potions we concoct, the more we can trade with average people . . . and the happier everyone is. It's a win-win situation. Plus . . . there's a lot more to it."

"Like the bad magic?"

Witchling Two's glance darkened. "We deal out

punishments, too. We're in charge of making sure that everything is fair."

"But there's the justice system. What about that?"

"Consider us the catchall. We never let any crime go unpunished, even if your human justice system lets people go. That's why people are afraid of us."

"But what sort of crimes?"

"All sorts of crimes, any sorts of crimes. We pick and choose."

"So it's all pretty random then? That doesn't seem fair. Or is it fair?"

Witchling Two frowned. "Yes . . . no . . . maybe . . . whether it's fair or not, it *does* keep people on their best behavior."

"Hmm," Rupert said.

"Remember, don't tell anyone!"

"Who am I going to tell?" Rupert said. "I won't tell anyone as long as you don't tell my mom that I'm a witch's apprentice."

Witchling Two giggled. She took another sip of hot chocolate. "You're thinking about something," she said solemnly. "Your face is all scrunched like a raisin."

"A raisin?"

She nodded. "Your forehead is all squiggly. Out with it!"

"Can a witch be anyone?" Rupert said. "Anyone at all?"

"What do you mean?"

"I . . . I think Mrs. Frabbleknacker is a witch," Rupert said.

Witchling Two opened and shut her mouth wordlessly. "Tell me everything."

So Rupert told her all about Mrs. Frabbleknacker—from the day he first started fifth grade to the field trip at the dump, from the day she forbid everyone from talking to the latest vocabulary lesson. He told Witchling Two every single detail. Once he started talking, it was impossible to stop, and Witchling Two was a good listener, nodding and gasping at all the right moments.

When Rupert was done, she took a sip of hot chocolate and frowned. "There's just one problem . . . there *is* no Freckleneckle Witch."

"Frabbleknacker," Rupert corrected. "She must be using a fake name."

"But why would a witch become a teacher?"

"I don't know," Rupert said. "Maybe she's bored

with the Witches Council. Or maybe she just wants to torture innocent children."

"Have you told your mom about this?"

"She doesn't believe me. No one does," Rupert said.

"Huh," she said as she swirled her hot chocolate. "Something about this situation is rabbit!"

"Is *what?*"

"Rabbit! It's when something doesn't smell right."

"You mean, something's *fishy*," Rupert corrected.

Witchling Two ignored him. "Well, I believe you, Rupert," she said firmly. She reached across the table and patted his hand. "I believe in you, and I believe you."

Plan B

On Sunday, only a week and a half before Witchling Two's Bar Exam, Rupert called for an emergency practice session.

Witchling Two snuck in through the basement window, carrying her enormous witching textbook. She also brought a backpack, stuffed to the brim with an encyclopedia of magic, a magical history textbook, four potions books, three spell books, two witch crime novels, and five dozen lollipops.

"I'm impressed you fit all this in your bookbag," Rupert said.

"I bewitched it to hold everything."

"*You* bewitched it?" Rupert said.

Witchling Two stuck two cream-soda-flavored lollipops in her mouth. "I did . . . or Nebby."

"So it was Nebby then?"

Witchling Two smiled guiltily.

Rupert sat down on an old, worn chair and folded his legs so that he was cross-legged. "Okay," he said. "Welcome to magic boot camp."

"Camp?" Witchling Two said eagerly, jumping on a sofa chair next to Rupert.

"Yes, camp."

"Are you my counselor?"

"Sure," Rupert said. "Now first order of busi—"

"Will there be *s'mores*? And roasted marshmallows? And campfire songs? And—"

"Only if you *focus* and show signs of improvement."

Witchling Two clamped a hand over her mouth and nodded vigorously.

"Pass me your textbook," Rupert said. He started with potions because that was her best subject. If he could just get her confident about her magical abilities then maybe—just maybe—she'd be able to perform a spell right.

He asked her about potion ingredients, how long to brew particular potions, which potions are best for which occasion, and what sorts of potions are legally acceptable to use on other witches. She aced question after question, and the smile on her face grew wider and wider. Finally, Rupert realized that they needed to move on and practice something she wasn't so comfortable with.

"Okay, now let's practice for your WHAT," Rupert said.

"WHATs."

"What?"

"WHATs."

Rupert scratched his head. "Haven't we already had this conversation?"

"Perhaps," said Witchling Two. "Ask away, Mr. Counselor. I want my 'mallows!"

Rupert thumbed through the pages. He stopped almost immediately when a question caught his eye.

He passed the book to Witchling Two and they stared at it together:

A human is found wandering the Witches Council lair. What do we do with him?

A. Boil his toes.

B. Broil his foes.

C. Soil his clothes.

D. Oil his nose.

Witchling Two hummed. "Umm . . . is it D?"

"No, sorry, A."

"Ooh, so close! That was my fourth pick after D, C, and then B."

"Let's try another one," Rupert said.

Historically, witches were drawn to the town of Gliver-stoll in particular because . . .

A. We heard rumors that the area was full of fruitful potion ingredients.

B. We wanted to build our tower on the highest known peak in the world.

C. The Earth called out to us, and we felt our magic surge.

D. We felt it would be pretty to live by the ocean.

"I know this one!" Rupert said. "Which means, you must know it, too."

"I must?"

"You told me the other day," Rupert said. "Remember? When we made hot chocolate?"

"Oh, yes!" Witchling Two said. She scratched her head. "Ummm . . ." Rupert handed her a pencil, and she chewed on the eraser. Then she flung it over her shoulder and grabbed another pencil. She chewed

114

and discarded, chewed and discarded. She ate five erasers before Rupert stopped her by putting a hand on her shoulder.

"You can do this. I know you know it. You're just scaring yourself. When you're looking at these questions, just pretend you're talking to me. Now, I just asked you about the history of Gliverstoll, and you say—"

"C."

"Yes!"

"I GOT ONE! I GOT ONE!" she shouted, throwing a handful of lollipops into the air like confetti. She pointed at A. "See that? Answer A explains why some of the witches went to Foxbury. And answer B shows why some of the witches went to Harkshire. The ancient witches were split three ways, you see, so we divided. But I still think that Gliverstoll holds all the most powerful witches. The Fairfoul Witch is the most feared and mighty of all the witches in every town. I mean, witchlings from Foxbury and Harkshire even come *here* to become Bar Exam certified witches. Gliverstoll is a big deal."

"Huh," Rupert said. He thought of all the places that didn't have witches—like Butterly, where his aunt and uncle lived. "And why didn't the witches go anywhere else? Why didn't they go to Butterly, for example?"

The witchling crinkled her nose. "Butterly! What in the *world* is in Butterly?"

Rupert shrugged.

"Well, like this question says, there was something about Gliverstoll that made us stronger and made our magic sharper. We all would have stayed here, but the other witches were just a stubborn pack of coots who were determined to go to Foxbury to pick up potions materials in the forest there. But then, all the witches in Foxbury began to fight, and so a group of them broke off and settled on top of the tallest peak in Harkshire. But they're just satellite colonies. Smaller and less powerful. Always looking to us for help."

"That must feel good—being part of the most powerful pack of witches."

"Sure!" Witchling Two said. "But I think it'd feel better if I actually became a real witch. I'm starting to get very nervous!"

"Okay, let's focus," Rupert said. He looked down at the textbook and read aloud.

According to witch customs, the appropriate first response to a duel request is . . .

A. Throw down white gloves.

B. Bow with your head hanging low.

C. Say, "I wholeheartedly and honorably accept your request, by the names of past witches long fallen and forgotten."

D. Shake your booty.

"B?" Witchling Two said.

Rupert looked at the answer key. "No, it's D . . . but that seems so odd."

Witchling Two scratched her head. "I don't think I've ever heard of a duel in my entire life. They happened, like, a gorilla years ago."

Rupert flipped the book to the copyright page. "No wonder—this book is two hundred years old! These questions must be *ancient*."

"Maybe that's why I'm getting so many wrong," she said glumly.

"If only we could get our hands on some more recent questions," Rupert said. "Then we'd know what sort of stuff they ask nowadays."

Witchling Two jumped up and began to giggle like a maniac. When she finally calmed down she sunk into her seat again and grinned. "Rupert, I'm thinking about something dangerous—something really risky." She put her mug on the table and looked at him with a glint of naughtiness in her eyes. "The witches have these files where they keep some of the old exams. What if we . . . took a peek? Just to see what the questions are like nowadays."

"That's not cheating, right?" Rupert said.

Witchling Two gasped. "On my honor, I would *never*! These questions are from past exams, Rupert, not the present one. It's like retrieving a study guide. If I'm going to pass this exam, I need to know what they've asked more recently than two hundred years ago, don't you think?"

Rupert nodded. "It would be helpful. But what does looking at these exams involve?"

"Sneaking into the Witches Council lair and reading through files that you—a human—and I—a witchling—are both forbidden to see."

"And if we get caught? Didn't that WHATs question *just* say that the punishment for humans wandering the witches lair is boiling my toes?"

"That, or seventy years of pain and torture. Maybe even death. Depends on how the head witch is feeling, but we may be able to butter her up with lollipops. *Anyone* can be buttered up with lollipops."

Rupert grimaced.

"Don't worry, Rupert! I'll keep you safe! I promise!" She looked down at her feet. "It's just . . . Gliverstoll is my home. I *can't* be exiled and drained of my magic. The exam is getting closer, and I'm not getting any better. And I'd really love your help."

The punishments were scary sounding, but Witchling Two had promised to protect him. He had to trust her. And he knew, deep down, that that this might be his only opportunity to save his best friend.

"Let's do it," Rupert said, and that was that.

The Worstest Assignment Ever

AT SCHOOL THE NEXT DAY, RUPERT WALKED INTO the classroom, and to his surprise, Bruno had finally figured out how to stack the toothpicks in a perfect tower. It took him almost two weeks, and over the course of those weeks, poor Bruno had lost about five pounds. He looked delirious.

Of course, when Mrs. Frabbleknacker entered the classroom, all the toothpicks immediately blew to the ground. Bruno pulled at his hair with his fingers, looking as though he might explode. But Mrs. Frabbleknacker ignored him.

"Children," she said, as though she was saying something truly awful like *Eye Gunk* or *Tuna Milkshake*. "Today is a day for science."

Rupert sat up straight in his seat and tried to look as ordinary and calm as possible. Over the months, Rupert had observed that Mrs. Frabbleknacker usually didn't notice when kids were being ordinary and calm. She only seemed to call on kids who looked nervous or frightened. And she only seemed to torture the kids who talked out or answered incorrectly. Rupert knew that the more ordinary he looked, the less likely it was that she would call on him, which made it less likely for him to be wrong, which made it less likely for him to be tortured.

"How about an experiment?" Mrs. Frabbleknacker said.

She put three glasses on the table and retrieved three thermoses from her bag. She tilted the thermoses and poured into each of the glasses. Each liquid was a different color and consistency. The first was dark and chunky, and it resembled black curdled milk. The second liquid was smooth looking, but it glowed a frightening shade of neon yellow. The third smelled. Really badly. Even from half-a-classroom's-length away, Rupert caught the whiff of skunk and sweaty sock mixed together. The third liquid was also so thick that it got stuck in the thermos. Mrs.

Frabbleknacker had to knock on the bottom of the thermos to coax the liquid out.

She licked her lips and looked around the room.

Don't look at me, don't look at me! Rupert thought.

"Hal!" Mrs. Frabbleknacker said.

The boy who sat behind Rupert walked to the blackboard.

"Manny!"

The boy who sat in front of Rupert walked to the blackboard.

Mrs. Frabbleknacker walked up to Rupert, but Rupert continued looking straight ahead. She bent down over his desk, and Rupert could feel the beads of sweat start to form on the back of his neck. He was more frightened than he had ever been in his life, but he was determined not to show emotion. He looked straight ahead. He held his breath. He didn't blink, not even when Mrs. Frabbleknacker blew banana breath in his face to make his eyelids tremble. She banged her fist on his desk, but Rupert did not move one nanometer.

Then, Mrs. Frabbleknacker took a huge whiff of air. Rupert was certain that she was about to send him to the front of the classroom, but then the strangest and most amazing thing happened—Mrs. Frabbleknacker's nostrils twitched, and she recoiled away from him.

"Allison Gormley!" she shouted.

A nervous Allison Gormley took her place at the front of the classroom, her knees knocking.

"Now, class," Mrs. Frabbleknacker said. "All of these potions come directly from the witches, and these drinks contain horrible chemicals that may seriously injure, harm, maim, wound, hurt, disfigure, mutilate, mar, or even kill your classmates. But just remember, this is science. And science must be explored. Sometimes, for the purpose of knowledge, we must sacrifice brave little boys and girls in order to make scientific progress. So Hal, Manny, Allison—we all thank you for volunteering."

Hal, Manny, and Allison exchanged glances that seemed to say *but we didn't volunteer!* Mrs. Frabbleknacker walked to the front of the room and hovered over the three trembling students. "Pick your poison," she said gleefully.

Allison quickly nabbed the black curdled milk, looking quite pleased with herself.

Hal cautiously picked up the neon yellow drink.

Which left Manny with the thick, smelly drink.

"Down the hatch, Allison," said Mrs. Frabbleknacker.

Allison tipped her glass up and gulped down the drink. When she was done, she slammed her glass on the table and wiped her mouth with her arm. She grinned and raised her hands above her head—she was a hero! A champion!

And then came the tiniest noise, so small it was almost impossible to hear.

Twoinggggg.

A hair sprouted on Allison's chin. She froze in horror.

TWOINGGGGG. TWOINGGGGG. TWOINGGGGG.

Another hair sprouted. Then another. Then another. One after the other—until Allison had sprouted a full mustache and beard. She put her hands to her face, and the skin behind her new facial hair went completely ashen. Then Allison ran from the classroom crying. Again.

Mrs. Frabbleknacker nodded at Hal, who tenderly swirled the neon liquid in his glass and brought it to his lips. He pinched his nose and chugged the entire drink in a matter of seconds. He turned to the class with puckered lips, and Rupert thought—without a doubt—that Hal was going to hurl.

But when Hal opened his mouth, a glowworm popped out. Hal covered his mouth with his hands, and Rupert leaned in closer. He squinted just a little bit as he studied Hal's mouth.

Hal burped, and five glowworms jumped out. He turned to Mrs. Frabbleknacker and looked like he was trying to say something, but he just coughed up fifteen more glowworms. Hal grabbed his throat and ran out of the classroom, a trail of glowworms falling to the floor in his wake.

By this time, Manny's hands trembled around his tonic. For a split second, Rupert hoped that Manny would refuse to drink the smelly, thick liquid, but as soon as Mrs. Frabbleknacker looked at him, Manny turned his glass upside down. Five minutes later, the thick liquid finally touched his lips. Ten minutes later, Manny had downed the entire skunky, sweat-scented juice.

He looked positively ordinary for a moment. Then one of his arms began to shrink. Then the other arm. Then his legs and torso. And with a small *HISS*, Manny's head became the size of an apple.

Mrs. Frabbleknacker swooped down and pinched Manny between her two fingers. She held him far away, as though he reeked. Then she dropped him in a glass jar and screwed the cap tight. Mrs. Frabbleknacker poked holes in the top with scissors and put the glass jar on the windowsill, ignoring the tiny high-pitched shouts and the soft thumps of Manny's fists on the glass.

"Class," Mrs. Frabbleknacker said, picking up a writhing glowworm off the floor and crushing it between her fingers, "I want you to write a five-hundred-thousand-word essay on glowworms to be handed to me next week."

No one said anything.

"And if it's not on my desk in exactly one week, you *all* will participate in science next time."

A Potion to Beat All Potions

WHEN RUPERT GOT HOME FROM SCHOOL, WITCH-
ling Two was busy cutting up the rhubarb from her
collection of ingredients. She hardly even looked up
when Rupert came in.

"Guess what?" she said.

"What?"

"There's a Council meeting tomorrow!"

"Uh . . . great?"

Witchling Two put down her dicing knife. "You
know what this means?" she said, grinning.

"That . . . the witches are going to meet?"

"Nope. Well, yes . . . but nope! It *means* that we're
going to be able to sneak into the Witches Council
lair tomorrow!"

Rupert perked up. "Really?"

"Of course, sillyshorts! If they're in a Council meeting, all of them will be occupied for forty minutes, and we'll get a peekity peek at those WHATs."

"Tomorrow!" Excitement—or nervousness—was churning in his stomach.

"Yes, yes. The day after this one," Witchling Two said. "Hold your britches—"

"Horses," Rupert corrected.

"Right!" she said. "In the meantime, help me with this potion, will you?"

Rupert shed his jacket, snapped on some latex gloves, and walked over to where Witchling Two was chopping with a very sharp kitchen knife. "What do you want me to do?"

"First, tell me a story."

"A story?" Rupert said. He tried to remember one of the bedtime stories his mother used to tell him, but the only one he could think of was *Runny Bunny Steals Your Money,* the story of a kleptomaniac bunny who sneaks into houses in the night and runs away with humans' wallets in his mouth. Somehow, he thought Witchling Two might not appreciate that one.

"Yes, a story. Tell me what Mrs. Fribbleknickers did today—you're looking off."

Rupert leaned against the table and explained the day's events to Witchling Two, recounting every detail of the poisonous potions that he could remember. As he talked, he held open a plastic bag for Witchling Two as she shoveled the rhubarb into it.

"Hmm," Witchling Two said, when Rupert had finished speaking. "She really *does* seem like a witch, doesn't she? Sounds like she had some really powerful juice." She wiped her hands on her floral apron. "Speaking of powerful juice, Rupert, I think we're ready to brew our first potion together."

Rupert smiled. They still hadn't brewed any potions yet. Instead, he and Witchling Two hunted for ingredients and organized them into boxes and jars every day. Now that Witchling Two finally wanted to make a potion, Rupert felt a squirmy sensation in his stomach. Part nervousness, part thrill.

"What kind of potion do you want to make?" Rupert asked.

"I don't know," Witchling Two said. "What do *you* want to make? We could do a sleeping potion, a forgetfulness potion, a flying potion, an invisibility potion, a brain-switch potion, or an egg salad potion, if you want."

"What's an egg salad potion?"

"A potion that tastes like egg salad."

"Why would I want that?" Rupert paused. Something was nagging at him. "Actually, I don't know if I even have time to help you," he said. "Mrs. Frabbleknacker assigned a five-hundred-thousand-word essay, due next week."

Witchling Two wrinkled her nose. "That's a lot of words. I think. That's probably like ten dictionaries worth of words. Or even a *penguin*'s worth!"

"Is that a lot?"

She nodded vigorously.

Rupert slumped down at the table and took out a notebook and pen. "Start working on whatever potion you want, and I'll join you later." Rupert tapped his pencil against his notebook. Then he tapped it against his teeth, enjoying the clicky noise of clatter-bumping. Then he tapped it against his head, which is a proven way to get your brain to move faster.

Then he got a burst of inspiration and started scribbling:

Glowworms by Rupert Campbell

There are many kinds of worms. One type is a glow-worm. They glow. There are also wiggly worms. And fat worms. And squirmy worms. Those are the kind my mom hates. There are long worms and short worms. If you cut a worm in half, it becomes two worms. If you cut a worm in thirds, it becomes three worms. But you shouldn't cut worms because they have feelings, too. You also shouldn't step on a worm because it will smush on your shoe, and it will take a long time to clean its guts off. Worms are not spaghetti.

Rupert counted the words. One hundred. He only had four hundred ninety-nine thousand nine hundred words to go.

He wrote another sentence, and frowned. How in the world was he going to write so much about worms? He was already running out of things to say.

He felt Witchling Two's hand on his shoulder, and when he looked up at her face, she was leaning over him, craning to see what he was writing. She made a *hmmm* noise and crumpled her nose again.

"You got that part from me," she said, pointing at the part Rupert had just written. Rupert leaned over his paper and read the last few sentences over again:

Do you ever notice that words sound funny if you say them too many times? Especially Worm. Worm, worm, worm, worm, worm, worm, worm, worm, worm, worm, worm, worm, worm, worm, worm, worm.

"Well I'm just trying to fill up space," Rupert said. "Five hundred thousand words . . ." he said wistfully.

Witchling Two banged her hands on the table, and Rupert jumped. Then she threw her head back and cackled, as all good witches do. Rupert patiently waited while she laughed so hard that she lay on the table and panted. He was starting to grow fond of her surprises—she always said the oddest things and never did what Rupert expected her to do. That was one of the reasons he loved being her apprentice.

When Witchling Two stopped panting, Rupert said, "Why are you laughing like that?"

"Because!" she said. "Put your books away— you're going to help me with this potion."

"What about my paper?" Rupert asked.

"Don't write it . . . you won't have to." Witchling

Two tied her hair up in a ponytail. "We're brewing something to help you with Mrs. Frabbleknocker."

Rupert walked over to her cauldron and peered inside. It was big, copper, deep, and completely empty.

"What do we need?" Rupert asked.

Witchling Two put a hand to her temple—in serious-beyond-serious thought. "We're going to need some of the ingredients I brought from my special supply. Hmm . . . we'll need . . . a goose egg! Aaaaaand a moose leg! Aaaaaand a loose peg!"

Rupert fetched a goose egg from a cardboard box and an enormous moose leg from a giant jar in the corner of the room—though he was almost too horrified to touch the preserved leg. It was extremely heavy, and Witchling Two needed to help him drag it across the basement. Eventually, with her help, he threw both the egg and the leg into the cauldron. "What is a loose peg?" Rupert asked. "I don't think we have any of those."

Witchling Two walked over to a stool in the corner of the basement, flipped it over, and wiggled the legs. On the third try, the leg creaked. Witchling Two hoisted the stool above her head, marched over to the cauldron, and tossed the entire chair in.

Then she grabbed a canoe paddle from Rupert's mother's old boat and stirred the potion until it started to crackle. Rupert and Witchling Two stood over the sizzling, sputtering, spitting cauldron. It hissed and coughed like a choking possum. Witchling Two dipped a finger into the dark oily potion and stuck her finger in her mouth.

"Delicious! Like cabbages in gravy! With a hint of pickles."

Rupert cringed. "Are you sure this is safe to drink?"

"Positutely! I've brewed this one before with Nebby. It needs to sit for five days, but after that, it works great, I promise." Witchling Two dipped a ladle into the potion and scooped a cup into Rupert's empty water bottle. She pushed the potion into his arms with a wild grin. "Next Monday, make sure to take this right before Mrs. Frubblekunckle collects the papers. And think about her while you drink it."

"You aren't going to tell me any more than that?"

"You'll see," she said, in such a way that Rupert knew the conversation was closed.

Don't Smell the Flowers

THE NEXT DAY, SCHOOL WAS A NIGHTMARE. AT first, everyone was so nervous about their papers on glowworms that no one even paid attention to Mrs. Frabbleknacker as she taught about the psychology of phobias. But Mrs. Frabbleknacker noticed—and she wasn't happy. As punishment, Mrs. Frabbleknacker made Kaleigh read an entire novel in front of the class to cure her fear of public speaking, Francis sit in a janitor's closet all day to cure his fear of small spaces, and Allison coddle a tarantula to cure her fear of spiders. Allison ran from the classroom crying.

Rupert was glad when school was over. He went home immediately and changed into black clothing and packed his backpack with emergency items—a flashlight, a water bottle, a whistle, a first aid kit—just in case.

He looked at the clock—Witchling Two was already five minutes late.

Rupert began to pace around his room as he thought about her. He was starting to get more nervous for Witchling Two's Bar Exam than she was. They only had a week and three days until her exam, and she hardly seemed any better. Every time Rupert asked her to practice spells or her WHATs, she insisted on gathering ingredients or brewing. In only two days, they had brewed—and tested—fifteen successful potions, from flu-remedy potions, to hair-restoration potions, to sneezing potions, to tongue-twister potions, to flying potions—they had even made egg salad potion.

He knew Witchling Two just wanted to practice what she was good at, but he needed to do a better job at keeping her on task. She simply *had* to pass the WHATs and the spells portion of the exam—otherwise his only friend would be kicked out of Gliverstoll forever.

He tapped his pencil nervously on every object he

encountered until Witchling Two popped up by his window. Rupert ran to let her in, and she toppled into the room with a goofy grin.

"Lair, lair, lair, lair! Lair, lair, lair, lair! Luh-luh-luh-lair, luh-lair! LAIR!"

"All right, all right," Rupert said. "I get it!"

"We have to start walking over there in a half hour," Witchling Two said. "That's when their meeting officially starts. We have to get in and out. No talking to anyone. No stopping to smell the flowers. In and out. Got it?"

"In and out," Rupert repeated. He twisted his hands. "Okay. Okay. This is going to be okay. We're going to be okay."

"*Okay?* We'll be great!"

Rupert fidgeted.

"So I've drawn a map of the Witches Council lair," she said, laying a drawing of two wiggly circles and a star on Rupert's bed. He laughed. It was the worst drawing he had ever seen.

"What is this?" Rupert asked.

"We'll start . . . here!" She pointed to the left edge of the paper. "Then we'll walk to there," she said pointing at the star. "Got it?"

"No," Rupert said, trying to make sense of the drawing.

Witchling Two jumped up. "Just follow me," she said. Rupert followed her downstairs, and he locked the door behind him. He wondered for a moment whether he should leave a note for his mom—she would be home in an hour and probably wonder where he went—but he decided that if he told her about his excursion to the Witches Council lair, he would have to tell her about his apprenticeship. And if he told her about his apprenticeship, his mother would forbid it, and Rupert wasn't ready to stop being Witchling Two's friend. So he left no note and hoped for the best.

Rupert followed Witchling Two down Piggleswumpfer Court to Yammerstop Way. He saw the fish-and-chips restaurant down the hill, and his eye gravitated to the giant boulder behind the restaurant—the boulder that could only be seen at this street, at this angle. Witchling Two grabbed Rupert by the collar and pulled him behind a lamp-post.

Rupert gulped, stuffing his hands in his pockets. "Why are we stopping?"

Witchling Two shook her head and pointed at the boulder.

"What is that?"

"That's where we're going," she said. "The Council meeting starts in platypus minutes."

"Do you know where we're going?"

Witchling Two flicked her hand. "Easy, peasy. When a witch turns ten, she's allowed to take a tour of the Council's lair for the first time. I know exactly where they have their meeting and exactly where they keep a record of all the WHATs. That's where we're headed—to the Filing Room!"

"Right," Rupert nodded.

"Stay close to me," Witchling Two said. "We can't get separated."

"Right."

"And remember, don't smell the flowers."

"Right, we're in a rush."

"Yes, but don't smell the flowers."

"Right," Rupert said. "Hurry. Yes. Got it."

"Yes, but don't smell the flowers."

Rupert stamped his foot. "Okay!" he said. "I got it already!"

Witchling Two smiled. "Good!" she said, and then she ran.

Rupert followed her as closely as he could, sticking to her back like sweat. Together, they ran down the rest of Yammerstop Way, past the row of coral houses. They ran past the playground (though Witchling Two stopped for a moment to put a handful of sand in a jar). They ran past the quilting store. They ran past Kaleigh's purple house (to which Witchling Two squealed, "Ooh! I want a house like that one!"). They ran past the fish-and-chips restaurant. And then they ran immediately left, to a grassy area where the boulder sat.

Rupert and Witchling Two panted for breath as they walked up to the giant rock. Witchling Two pressed her hand against the boulder, and it rolled aside, revealing an archway that led straight into the heart of the hill.

With two enormous gulps, they walked inside, and the boulder rolled back into place behind them. Rupert stared—the passageway had linoleum floors, pictures of fuzzy, smiling baby animals on top of powder blue wallpaper, and bright lights.

"This is . . . not what I expected," Rupert said.

Witchling Two grabbed his hand, and they briskly jogged down the hallway, which led into a domed room with twelve golden chandeliers. Cawing blackbirds flew across the room then rested on the arms of the chandeliers, peering down at Rupert and Witchling Two with their beady eyes. Across the domed room were two carved doors and an archway. Rupert wandered to the center of the circular room, where he could hear the echoes of voices.

"Ve haven't been ushering enough of ze tourists!" a gruff-sounding woman said. "Ze past month 'as been too slow on ze business."

"It's been fine," a soft but firm voice said. Rupert recognized the voice—it was Nebby. "I'm more concerned about Justice Column Forty-six. The amendment for this article is still up for debate."

"Pish posh!" said a nasally voice. "I'm more concerned about Witchling Two gallivanting with that human!"

"There is no reason to believe that she is still with the human," Nebby said coldly.

"We caught her! We chased her! How can you deny this?"

"That was one time. There is no evidence that

indicates she's still with the boy, and now you're spreading rumors and lies."

There was a hissing sound, then a gavel, then cries of *Order! Order!*

Witchling Two put a hand on Rupert's arm. "We don't have time for this," she whispered.

"They're talking about us," Rupert mouthed back.

She shrugged and walked toward the archway, beckoning for Rupert to follow her. They walked into an archway and found themselves in a tunnel made entirely of dirt. The cold air made Rupert shiver. For a while, he kept up behind Witchling Two, but he soon found himself slowing down until finally he stopped.

His nostrils twitched, and he sniffed. He smelled the most beautiful smell that anyone in the world had ever smelled.

"What is that?" he said. "What is that wonderful—"

He looked to the left and spotted a bed of flowers. He walked over to them and leaned closer. They were the most delicate shades of red, violet, pink, and indigo, and Rupert reached out to touch one . . .

Footsteps came closer from around the corner. *"What are you doing?"* shouted Witchling Two.

Rupert sniffed. "Come smell these!" he said. "They are splendid!"

"I told you *not* to smell the flowers!"

Rupert inhaled. "Oh, how glorious!" he said. "How wonderful! How magnificent! How astonishing!"

Witchling Two hoisted him up into a piggyback and began to run down the hallway with him. "I *told* you not to smell the flowers. Never trust a pretty flower. They are terribly sneaky things . . . as sneaky as bunnies."

Rupert twisted and turned, trying desperately to get out of her piggyback grip, but she held on to him tightly.

When she rounded the corner, she put him down. She dragged him down a torch-lit hallway, and with the flickering firelight, it was starting to look like a real witch's lair. Finally, they stopped at a wooden door.

Witchling Two whisked him into a small room with many stacks of crumpled up papers, and Rupert finally began to realize that the smell was gone— and he had a thundering headache.

"What *was* that?" he groaned. He felt groggy, like

he couldn't tell whether he was sleeping or awake, or what was up and what was down.

"Flowers," she said, shaking her head. "They're our security traps. We witches can't smell them, but they're meant to catch human intruders. They put you under a spell, and the moment you touch the flowers, you're caught in a net."

Rupert put his hand to his temple. "Thanks for rescuing me."

"I couldn't very well leave my apprentice at the mercy of a flower bed, could I?"

Rupert licked his lips, looking around the room. "So this is the Filing Room?"

"Sure is!"

"You call this filing?" Rupert said, staring at the stack of crumpled up papers on the floor. He looked around the room. There wasn't a filing cabinet in sight—just a whole bunch of papers on the ground and a small, wooden table by the door.

Witchling Two pulled a soggy piece of parchment out of a stack. She read it over with a *hmm,* then she crumpled it and tossed it over her shoulder before picking up a new piece of paper. Rupert walked over and began to read papers. They hardly made sense to him, and a lot of them had names of Gliverstoll townspeople and punishments on them.

"What are these?" Rupert asked, holding up a paper that read: *Viola Frobbleman punished under article 31. Caught vandalizing the bell tower. Punishment: Toecorn.* He shuddered at the thought of Toecorn.

"We keep everything all filed together, so we've got record on all the punishments we've ever given, the WHATs questions, witch evaluation reports, research notes, and witchling report cards all mixed together.

Rupert shook his head. At this rate, they'd *never* find what they were looking for. He dug through more papers, some soggy, some crusty, all smelling like sour eggs. There were more papers than Rupert thought—they were endless, circling the ground and piling up to his calves like a parchment swimming pool. There were far too many papers to possibly read in such a short span. But they had to try.

Witchling Two clicked her tongue. "We need to leave, Rupert," she said. "We have bobcat minutes to get out of here."

"One more minute," Rupert said as he dug into another stack. It wasn't right, and he tossed it aside.

He grabbed one, two, three—but none of them were right.

Witchling Two bit her nails. "Rupert . . ."

"You're going to have to do a spell," Rupert said, looking up from the parchment he was reading.

"A spell?"

"We've got to find those test questions! This is your only chance. All we've got is no time and a lot of magic. Just think of it as more practice for your exam."

Witchling Two took a deep breath. "I'll try," she said with a nod. She snapped her fingers. "I need the test papers. The test papers . . . the test papers," she breathed.

Suddenly a cloud of wispy smoke erupted from the ground. The room grew thick and foggy and muggy and damp.

"What did you do?" cried Rupert. "We needed test papers, not wet vapors!"

Witchling Two let out a sob. "I'll never pass!"

"Yes, you will," Rupert said, waving his hands to clear away some of the fog. "I'm going to help you study, even if we can't find current WHATs questions! Now, how much time do we have left before the Council meeting ends?"

"Catfish minutes—we really have to go!"

This trip was a failure, Rupert thought as he stood up, *but this room is so messy it's no wonder we couldn't find anything.* He grabbed Witchling Two's hand and pulled her through the vapors, which were now erupting in spurts. "Come on—let's get out of here!"

Witchling Two followed him but stopped dead just before the door. She walked to the wooden table in the corner.

"Come on!" Rupert said. "We have to get out of here!"

She gasped.

"Rupert!" She hovered over the table, and when she turned around, she held up a piece of parchment. "Your mom."

Rupert's heart leaped into his throat. "What?"

Witchling Two cleared her throat. *"Joanne Campbell punished under article nineteen. Caught stealing forbidden potions from the Witches—"*

"That's my mom!"

"But that's not everything!" she said, her face growing pale. "There's more. It says, *Punishment: Firstborn child.*"

Witchling Four

"WHAT DOES THAT MEAN? AM I A PUNISHMENT?"

"No," Witchling Two said. "I think it means . . . you belong to the witches. They've claimed you."

"B-but I *can't* belong to the witches. I'm not allowed to go near them! This doesn't make any sense."

Witchling Two scratched her head.

"Why was this file on the table?"

"Nebby and Storm—they knew you had become my apprentice. They must know that we didn't stop seeing each other after that day in the Brewery, and they must have wanted to read up on your family history."

He looked at the piece of paper again.

"What did she steal? What's a forbidden potion?"

"Oh, it could be lots of things. Love potion, death potion, revival potion, fertility potion, intelligence potion, obedience potion. The witches keep all sorts of potions that are forbidden for humans. For moral reasons."

He looked at Witchling Two quizzically, but she turned to her watch.

"Honeybee minutes!" she squealed.

She grabbed Rupert's hand, and the two of them sped down the hallways. They ran past the flowers so fast that Rupert didn't even have time to inhale. The entrance to the Dome Room was just ahead of them—and they leaped into the room like two gazelles.

"Well, well, well!" said a snotty-sounding voice. "Little miss witchling breaking *all* the rules."

Witchling Two froze, and Rupert turned around the room. Leaning against the wall was a short girl who looked well on her way to becoming the scariest witch Rupert had ever seen. She had tangled brown hair and small, squinty eyes. Her face was sharp and angular, her lips thin and curled. And as she grinned, she bared her small, jagged teeth.

"You brought a *human* inside the Witches Council

lair?" the small girl said, smacking her lips in delight. "Witchling Two, you're in so much trouble. I mean, they'll probably make you clean the dome with your tongue. You always do this, you know—make us *real* witches look bad. You're a joke—an insult to the name witch." The small girl cracked her neck. "And you could never pass your exam, not even if the entire Witches Council gave you private lessons. I don't know why you even try."

Witchling Two looked down. A blush crept on her freckly face, and she shuffled her feet.

Rupert squeezed her hand. "Go on," he whispered. "You're better than that! Now tell her off."

Witchling Two looked up and beamed. "Hello, Witchling Four!" she said.

Witchling Four looked nervous at Witchling Two's sudden change of attitude. "Did you hear what I just said? You're getting in trouble! They'll never let you take the exam, and you and your *niceness* will be banished forever," she said, wrinkling her nose at the word *niceness,* as if there was no worse insult in the world.

"Wait . . . are you threatening to tattle on her?" Rupert said.

Witchling Four nodded.

"You wouldn't," Witchling Two said. "You can't—because if you tell, you'll have to admit that you were here, too. And then you'll be in just as much trouble."

The sound of a gavel and cries of *Meeting Adjourned!* echoed throughout the room. Rupert tugged on Witchling Two's sleeve in panic. She nodded toward his backpack, and Rupert handed it over to her.

"At least *I* didn't bring a human in here!" Witchling Four shouted.

"Human?" Witchling Two said, reaching deep into the backpack. She pulled out the jar full of sand and handed Rupert back the bag. She smiled as she twisted the cap of the jar open. "I don't see a human. Do you see a human?" she said to Rupert.

Rupert caught on fast. "I don't see anything!"

Rupert closed his eyes and his mouth, and Witchling Two dumped the jar of sand all over Rupert's head.

Witchling Four's eyes slid off him, and Rupert and Witchling Two dashed toward the boulder. They ducked around the corner and hid for a moment so that they didn't make too much noise as they scurried toward the exit. Behind him, he heard the doors open and a few witches cry, "Witchling Four! You naughty child!"

"Quick!" Witchling Four shouted. "Witchling Two is here with a human boy!"

"Quiet, you! Stop spreading rumors and lies," said a squeaky voice. "I'm so ashamed of you right now! You know you're not supposed to be here!"

"But Coldwind!" Witchling Four whined.

"No buts, bums, bottoms, tushes, tails, rears, fannies, or glutei maximi, missy! You've brought me shame and humiliation. No saliva slushie for you tonight!"

Witchling Two tugged on Rupert's sleeve, and he tiptoed behind her as they made their way through the passageway with the framed smiling animals. At last, they made their way to the boulder, and it sat just ahead of them—but then the lights flicked off, and they were stuck in darkness.

"What happened?" Rupert whispered, frightened. "Are they gone?"

"No, it's our new environmental conservation plan. They like to turn off the lights when this portion of the hallway isn't being used. We're very concerned about the environment, too."

"But why aren't the witches leaving the lair? Isn't their meeting over?"

Witchling Two giggled. "We were really lucky Witchling Four was there—they're dealing with her in the punishing room. Now let's get out of here."

And she dragged Rupert toward the exit.

Secrets, Secrets Are No Fun . . .

THEY SCAMPERED UP YAMMERSTOP WAY AND didn't stop until they were just outside Rupert's house. Then they leaned on his porch for support and panted.

"We were almost toast!" Rupert said.

"And they didn't even suspect that anything was rabbit!"

Rupert shook his head. "Fishy. That rabbit thing will never catch on," he said. "But anyway, who was that girl? Witchling Four?"

Witchling Two went pale and started stammering. "Well, you see, um, er, uh, erm . . ."

"She was horrible. An absolute nightmare. Is that why you won't practice with the other witchlings? That's why you hired me, isn't it?"

"No, I really thought you would be useful with your, erm, ability to do things non-magically . . ."

"Tell the truth."

"Okay, fine," Witchling Two said. "I don't really get along with the other witchlings. I guess you could tell that I'm a bit . . . different, and they make fun of me a lot. And I was . . . I was . . . I was . . ."

"Lonely," Rupert finished for her.

Witchling Two nodded.

Rupert understood that feeling quite well.

Except at that moment, for the first time in a long time, Rupert didn't feel lonely at all. When he looked at Witchling Two and thought about all their crazy misadventures, he actually felt a lot better. And even though he hadn't known her for that long, and even though she was a bit batty, and even though they weren't supposed to be friends, she was the best friend Rupert had ever had.

The screen door flew open, and Rupert's mother burst out with two bowls of ice cream. "Hello, kids! Would you like a treat? Or if you don't want this, I can make you something microwavable."

Witchling Two's eyes narrowed, and she crinkled her nose. "What is that?"

"Mr. and Mrs. Gummyum's homemade carrot ice cream."

Witchling Two's jaw dropped, and she wore a horrified expression. *"Carrot?"* she said. "Carrot ice cream?"

"Yes, dear. Try a spoonf—"

"B U U U N N N Y Y Y Y Y Y Y Y Y Y Y ! A A A A A A A A H H H H H H H H H H H H H H H H H H H H H - H H H H !" she screamed, bolting all the way down Piggleswumpfer Court and out of sight.

"Your friend is an odd little duckling," his mother said.

Rupert shrugged.

His mother sat down on the porch step, and Rupert crawled next to her. They began to eat the ice cream in silence, just enjoying the warmth of the sun and the hush of the ocean and the crispness of the salty air.

But Rupert wasn't feeling that hungry, and after a few bites, he put down his bowl. Sitting next to his mom reminded him of what he saw in the witches' lair—the horrible realization that he now belonged to the witches because of something his mom had done many years ago.

"Mom . . . What did you steal from the witches?" He didn't mean to say it, but it just sort of burbled out of him.

His mother's spoon flew out of her hand, and she scurried to pick it up again. "What?" she said. "What did you say?"

"What did you steal?"

"How could you possibly know that?" she whispered.

Rupert froze. How could he be so stupid? Of *course*, she'd want to know how he knew . . . but he couldn't tell her about Witchling Two or their trip into the witches' lair.

His mother put down her bowl. "Rupert?" When he didn't answer her, his mother's eyes began to water.

She began to cry, and she pulled him close to her, holding him tight. He hugged her back and tried to comfort her, but it was hard when he didn't understand why she was crying.

When she calmed down, he tried again, "What did you take, Mom?"

She hugged her knees and stared off into the sea. "This is important—which witch have you been talking to, Rupert?"

"None of them! Honest!" And it was the truth. Technically, Witchling Two wasn't a witch . . . yet. Rupert took a deep breath. "I was walking near Digglydare Close, and I overheard two witches talking," he paused. "But I didn't talk to them, and I wasn't *on* the witch street."

"But you were lingering by it?" She took his hand. "Don't *ever* do that again," she scolded, but it sounded more like pleading. "How many times have I told you, stay *away* from that side of town."

"Why?" Rupert said. "Why do I have to stay away from the witches? And what did you steal? And why did you do it? And why do we stay in Gliverstoll if you hate the witches so much? Why do you keep all these secrets?"

She stood up and walked over to the porch swing. "I'm trying to protect you, Rupert."

"I don't want that. I just want answers."

When it was clear she wasn't going to discuss the witches any longer, he walked into the house. For hours, he listened to his mother rocking back and forth in her porch chair. When he finally went to bed, she was still rocking.

Turning in the Essay

ON MONDAY, FOUR DAYS BEFORE WITCHLING Two's exam, Rupert walked into class with 200 words of his 500,000 word essay. He clutched his paragraph in his right hand and a water bottle of emerald glossy potion that Witchling Two had made him in his left. He'd let the potion sit for five days, and it was ready for use . . . whatever it did. Witchling Two still wouldn't tell him what potion she had brewed for him, and knowing her, he had no idea what to expect. He felt like he was going to vomit.

He looked to his left and saw Kyle Mason-Reed struggling to keep his stack of spiral notebooks from toppling. Rupert thought that he must have used twenty-five notebooks—he tried to count, but he kept messing up the numbers. Rupert looked to his right and saw an exhausted-looking Allison Gormley. Rupert had overheard Kaleigh whisper to Millie just before class that Allison's facial hair from Mrs. Frabbleknacker's potion had fallen out five hours after she had taken the potion, but until then Allison had spent the day hiding in the bathroom stall, wailing that she was going to have to join a circus. And Rupert had overheard Bruno tell Francis that Hal had stopped vomiting worms one hour after he drank the potion. Rupert was relieved that at least Allison and Hal were back to normal. Manny, unfortunately, was still trapped in his jar on the windowsill.

But Manny's punishment was nothing compared to what Rupert feared would happen to him today.

He looked at Allison again. She stroked her neat stack of typed printer paper. Her pile was even taller than Kyle's, and Allison sat straight in her seat, looking rather pleased with herself.

Rupert looked around the rest of the classroom. His classmates looked positively ghoulish: pale skin, droopy eyes, solemn faces. A few people struggled to stay awake, and Rupert watched as Hal and Kaleigh slept with their chins tucked to their chests—and then violently jerked their heads upward to wake themselves.

Rupert felt completely out of place. He was the only well-rested one *and* the only one who hadn't done the assignment. Everyone—Allison, Kyle, Kaleigh, Hal, Millie, Francis, and even Bruno—was fiddling with a giant pile of papers. Rupert placed his single sheet of paper on his desk with a sickly wince.

Mrs. Frabbleknacker kicked the door open. "Children," she said, as though she was saying something truly awful like *Morning Breath* or *Snot Pudding*. "Today is a very special day. A day of science for *some*," she looked straight at Rupert's desk.

Rupert gulped. His hands clutched his water bottle even tighter.

Mrs. Frabbleknacker walked down the first row of students, her shoes clip-clopping in time with Rupert's nervous pulse. He looked away from Mrs. Frabbleknacker for a quick moment, and his gaze rested on Manny, who was calmly nibbling a leaf inside his jar on the windowsill.

"Too few words," Mrs. Frabbleknacker said as

she walked past Bruno's desk. She picked up Bruno's essay and whacked him on the head with it. "Too many words," Mrs. Frabbleknacker said as she walked past Allison's desk. She punched Allison's papers, and the entire stack fell with a *swoosh* all over the floor. Allison blinked in disbelief. Then she ran from the classroom crying.

Rupert used the distraction as the perfect opportunity to bring the water bottle up to his lips and gulp down a few sips of Witchling Two's potion. He thought intensely about Mrs. Frabbleknacker—about the way she terrified him with every clomping step, the way she made every lesson into a dangerous task, and the way he would never ever smell bananas or belly-button lint in quite the same way again. When Rupert had taken five glugs, he quickly lowered the bottle and licked his lips. The potion tasted like bubble gum and mint and cinnamon all mixed together, like extra tangy mouthwash. Which was not what he was expecting, since Witchling Two had said it tasted like cabbages and gravy.

Rupert brought the bottle down to his knees and watched as scribbly handwriting suddenly appeared

on the side of the water bottle. *Sand Potion*, it said.
Rupert had no idea what that was—or what that
could even be.

He slipped the water bottle in his backpack and
waited for something amazing to happen. But the
problem was that Rupert didn't *feel* any different.
No tingles, no fuzzies, no change whatsoever. And
that was a problem because Mrs. Frabbleknacker
was right behind him, and he had no backup plan.

Mrs. Frabbleknacker flicked a match and lit
Manny's notebooks on fire. She threw her head back
and laughed until his essay crumbled into dusty ash.
Then she turned to Rupert.

Rupert clutched his two hundred words with both
hands, trembling. Mrs. Frabbleknacker hovered above
him, her long neck twisted like a floor lamp. Slowly
and meekly, Rupert looked up into her eyes.

Mrs. Frabbleknacker's eyes slipped and stumbled—her gaze was glued to the floor. She tried
to bring her eyes upward to meet Rupert, but she
couldn't keep her eyes locked on him. She grew
redder and redder—the more she tried to look at
Rupert and realized she couldn't—and madder and
madder.

Her thin lips twisted into an ugly snarl, and her pointy nose cringled up.

"RUPERT CAMPBELL!" she shouted, looking like she was about to pop. Her voice echoed throughout the classroom. Kyle leaned over and patted Rupert's hand sadly. *I'll always remember you fondly,* his expression seemed to say.

Mrs. Frabbleknacker grabbed the edge of Rupert's desk, but Rupert slipped out the side just before she threw the desk against the wall. It broke into four pieces.

"Tell me class," Mrs. Frabbleknacker said, steaming. "One minute a lazybones little boy is sitting in his desk—and the next minute he's gone!"

Rupert's classmates looked at Mrs. Frabbleknacker as though she was insane. Rupert inched against the chalkboard with a finger to his lips, warning his classmates not to look at him or point him out.

"But you aren't gone, *are you?*" Mrs. Frabbleknacker spat. "*Rupert Campbell.* I may not see you, but I can smell you. I can hear you. And I can *feel* you—"

Mrs. Frabbleknacker lunged at the chalkboard, and Rupert dashed to the other side of the classroom. She caught hold of Rupert's shirt and grabbed it, but he pulled away, tearing his shirt in the process.

Rupert didn't waste a second—he burst from the classroom and ran down the hall. He didn't know if Mrs. Frabbleknacker was following him or not, but he didn't have time to turn around and find out. He needed more help and more protection than he had ever needed before. And there was only one person who could help him: Witchling Two.

Double Trouble

RUPERT LOCKED HIS FRONT DOOR BEHIND HIM, ran through the house, and panted in the doorframe of his basement.

"Rupert?" Witchling Two said. She popped up from behind the wooden table. "How did the potion work on Mrs. Frabblebabble?"

Rupert stomped over to her and slammed his hands on the table. "*HOW?* She's madder than ever!"

Witchling Two giggled. "I knew it would work. I am good at potions, even if I'm rubbish at spells. Speaking of which, how would you like to practice spells today? My Bar Exam is coming up in four days, and I'm no better off today than when I met you."

"We have bigger problems than your Bar Exam right now!"

Witchling Two pouted. "Well there's no need to shout," she said.

"I don't understand what you did to me anyway. A *sand potion*—what is that?" Rupert thought about the way Mrs. Frabbleknacker's eyes couldn't stay on him. Rupert's jaw dropped. "You made me slippery to the human eye . . . just like sand is slippery to witches! Does that mean Mrs. Frabbleknacker isn't a witch after all?"

"I didn't make you slippery to the human eye, silly," Witchling Two said. "Just to Mrs. Frubble-bubble's eyes. You *were* thinking about her when you took the potion, right?"

"Of course I was, but that's not the prob—"

CRASH.

The sound of broken glass rattled throughout the house.

"She's here!" Rupert hissed. "Mrs. Frab-bleknacker!" He scurried underneath the table and hid.

"I'll deal with her," Witchling Two said. "No Mrs. Fribbleknobber is going to mess with my apprentice!"

Rupert held his knees and sucked in a great big breath. He hoped, wished, and prayed that his evil teacher wasn't at the basement door. He wasn't sure what Witchling Two could do to fight her—after all, she still wasn't very good at spell-work—but he appreciated the thought.

He was doomed. Utterly and completely doomed.

Witchling Two gasped, and Rupert threw his hands over his ears to block out the worst from coming.

"W-what are you doing here?" Witchling Two said, her voice unnaturally high-pitched.

"I knew it!" a familiar voice crowed. Rupert peeked out from under the table—Witchling Two's guardians, Nebby and Storm, were lingering by the stairs, their hoods shrouding their faces. Rupert could only see Nebby's very disapproving frown and Storm's very gleeful grin.

"I knew it!" Storm shouted again, throwing her hood back to reveal her pointed, wrinkly face. "I knew it, I knew it, I knew it! I *told* you that our witchling was still seeing the humanling! I *told* you she had been gallivanting with this boy! I *told* you it would land us in nothing but trouble!"

Nebby removed her hood, too, and Rupert almost

168

winced when he saw her face. She was wearing the I'm-very-disappointed-in-you expression. Of all the faces a parent could make, Rupert knew that was the worst one.

"How long have you known?" Witchling Two squeaked.

"Oh, we've known for a while," Nebby said ominously. "And what's more, the Fairfoul Witch also knows, now. She is *furious*."

Witchling Two grew pale. Rupert watched her tongue flub around in her mouth, trying to wrap around the perfect words. "Fairfoul knows?" she squeaked.

Storm and Nebby nodded, and a knot tugged in Rupert's stomach.

"How?" Witchling Two asked.

"I don't know. It was very sudden. At the stroke of the Witching Hour, she stormed out of her lair shouting profanities about a boy named Rupert Campbell," Nebby said.

Storm nodded sagely. "Must have consulted the tea leaves this afternoon. Yes, yes, she must have."

"But when would she have found out?" Witchling

Two asked. "Everyone knows she sleeps all day."

"It doesn't matter," Nebby said. "What matters is that she knows."

"We should have stopped them, Nebby," Storm said, though she was glaring at Rupert and Witchling Two. "I *told* you we should have stopped them before Fairfoul found out!"

"Why didn't you?" Rupert said.

Nebby's swiveled her head to look at him, and for the first time, Rupert thought he saw some gentleness swimming behind her eyes. "She was improving— her potions were sharper, suddenly she was acing her practice WHATs, and she was confident. And," Nebby paused to put her hand on Witchling Two's shoulder, "parents want to see their witchlings happy, Rupert. And Witchling Two has never been happier."

Witchling Two nodded robustly.

"But now I see that indulging your friendship was a mistake."

"Why's that?" Rupert asked.

"Didn't you hear, boy?" Storm said. "The Fairfoul Witch is furious! Fairfoul! And if Fairfoul is furious, then the rest of the Witches Council is furious, too."

"You can't practice with this boy any longer," Nebby said. "The Witches Council knows his identity—you've put this boy at deep risk. Though, he was already in deep risk—now he's a walking time bomb."

"That's exactly why I can't leave him," Witchling Two said firmly. "I didn't leave Rupert when the witches smoked us out of Pexale Close. I didn't leave him when the Witches Council was chasing us. I didn't leave him when he was having problems with Mrs. Frocklebopper. And I won't leave him now."

Rupert grinned. They really were friends.

Nebby elbowed Witchling Two. "You sure have a sensitive spot for this boy, hmm?"

"Getting into trouble, all day and all night!" crowed Storm. Then she bent over and laughed uncontrollably until she hiccupped for breath.

Witchling Two cocked her chin upward, a defiant expression etched on her face. But when she spoke, her voice trembled. "Storm Witch, Nebulous Witch—I've never asked you for anything big before, but I need your help now. If the Fairfoul Witch finds us, Rupert and I are *both* cooked. We need a protection spell around Rupert's house, and I need you to cast it. So will you help me?"

"We are bound to the code of the Witches Council," Storm said. "Technically, the Witches Council is supposed to find you and punish the boy—and since Fairfoul is the highest ranking witch, we should not disobey."

Rupert grabbed Witching Two's hand. Were they going to have to fight their way out of the basement against her guardians? Would they turn him over to the Fairfoul Witch?

Nebby took a step closer, and Rupert took one backward.

Nebby paused and smiled softly. "Don't be scared, Rupert. Witchling Two means more to us than a Fairfoul Witch decree. You ought to know that by now." Nebby walked to Witchling Two and affectionately patted her head. "You are our witchling, our family—and we will protect you. At least—until we figure out a long-term plan for you, Rupert. As I said, you are in terrible danger. Storm and I need to do a little investigating within the Witches Council before we can figure out how best to handle your situation. Promise me you'll stay put until we return. We'll discuss your options then, okay?"

Rupert nodded. "All right, I promise."

The Storm Witch and the Nebulous Witch both closed their eyes.

"Protection! Invisibility! Safety!" they shouted together.

"Unlimited supply of chips!" Witchling Two added.

And then they all snapped their fingers.

Rupert cowered as the house shook and thousands of whips rained from the ceiling. The Storm Witch and the Nebulous Witch clicked their tongues disapprovingly and snapped their fingers—the whips disappeared.

"You, boy," the Storm Witch snorted. "If you're really going to help her train, then make sure she practices her spells. She'll never pass with ruddy magic like that."

Hiding Rupert

WHEN THE STORM WITCH AND THE NEBULOUS Witch left, Witchling Two sat with her elbows on the table and her face in her fists. "If the Fairfoul Witch knows who you are, then she's probably on her way here. And you're in big trouble."

"Good thing Storm and Nebby did a spell, then."

"Storm and Nebby put a protection spell around your house, which should hold out against the Fairfoul Witch, but I want to make sure that *you* are hidden." She inched toward him eagerly, her eyebrows raised and her mouth curved into a sly grin.

"No . . ." Rupert said. "No, no, *no!*"

"I just want to do one itty-bitty invisibility spell!"

"Not a chance!"

Witchling Two leaped to her feet. "Rupert, listen. You are as visible as a flamingo in a desert! I think I know the perfect spell. . . ."

"Get away from me with your spells!"

"Aww, come on. You told me I needed more practice, right?"

"But not on *me*! I'll let you do a potion," said Rupert. "That's *it*."

"No time for a potion," Witchling Two muttered. "Invisibility potions have to simmer for three days. And the sand potion has to sit for five days, remember?"

"Then, just shower me with sand! What about that?"

"We don't have any sand around right now. And besides, a spell will last longer."

"No," Rupert said. "A thousand million billion times no."

Witchling Two solemnly shuffled her feet. "I understand," she sniffed. "I suppose I'll just fail my Bar Exam now because my apprentice wouldn't let me try out any spells. In four days, they'll take away my magic and force me into exile, never to be seen again." She dramatically hid her face in her hands and whimpered.

"I *can't* let you do a spell on me! What would happen if you mess up?"

Witchling Two perked up. "But there's no way this one can go wrong! Rupert, I swear! I'm choosing a long phrase so my magic can't confuse itself and produce something that sounds similar."

Rupert snorted. This logic sounded wrong—so very wrong.

"Now hold still. This is foolproof."

"Hold on—I didn't say yes! Hey—"

Witchling Two snapped her fingers. "Make it so he can't be seen," she said. "Can't be seen. Can't be seen." She snapped again.

Rupert didn't dare open his eyes, but then, he didn't feel any different. *Maybe this is just like the potion,* he thought. *I don't feel any different, but it still works. Maybe I'm invisible—*

Witchling Two screamed.

Rupert opened his eyes and the first thing he saw were green hands. *His* green hands.

He ran for a mirror, and he stood in front of it, watching his face turn from a peachy color to a pale lime color to a deep emerald color. He looked like a giant fruit fly.

"WHAT DID YOU DO?" he shouted. "WHAT DID YOU DO TO ME?"

Witchling Two whimpered, pulling her hair over her head to hide her freckly face. "I said *can't be seen*," she said, cowering away from Rupert's glare. "But you're *turning green*."

"I can see that!" Rupert snapped. "I thought you said this was foolproof!"

"Well, I thought a longer sentence would do the trick . . . less chance of sounding like something else."

"That wasn't even a very long phrase, Witchling Two!"

She squeaked. "I'm sorry!"

Rupert threw his hands in the air. "Well, that's just great. Now I'm more visible than ever! Please tell me you can fix this!"

"I'll just call Nebby and Storm," Witchling Two said, reaching for the telephone. "They'll fix you right back to norm—"

BAM.

Even from the basement, Rupert and Witchling Two could hear the front door bang open.

The Name

WITCHLING TWO POINTED TO RUPERT AND THEN the table in frantic, jerking motions, which was her way of saying *Hide.*

Rupert held up his green arm and pointed to it, which was his way of saying *What am I supposed to do about my green skin?*

Witchling Two shook her head. *That doesn't matter right now.*

Rupert silently stomped his foot. *Of course it matters! I look like asparagus!*

Witchling Two smiled. *No, you look more like a string bean.*

Rupert cocked his head. *What's the difference?*

Witchling Two raised an eyebrow. *I don't actually know.*

The wooden step at the top of the basement stairs creaked.

Rupert ducked under the table and hid his head in his knees.

PLUNK came the sound of a foot on the steps.

PLUNK THUD came the sound of another two steps.

PLUNK THUD PLUNK THUD PLUNK THUD came the sound of someone climbing down all the basement stairs.

"I-I can't explain," Witchling Two said.

Under the table Rupert shook his head. She was supposed to say that she *could* explain, not that she couldn't.

Witchling Two cleared her throat. "M-Mrs. Campbell, I—"

Rupert froze in horror. The only thing worse than being found by the Fairfoul Witch was being found by his mother. She could *not* find out that he ran out of school early. She could *not* find out that he was Witchling Two's apprentice. But mostly, she could *not* find out that he had green skin.

"Why are you in my basement?" Rupert's mother asked. "What was your name again?"

"Erm," Witchling Two said.

Please, Rupert begged in his head. *Please, for pity's sake! Please don't say your name is Witchy!* He wiggled his toes, hoping that he could send Witchling Two his thought waves.

"Sandy," Witchling Two said. "My name is absolutely, positively, without a doubt Sandy. Sandy, Sandy, Sandy—it rolls nicely off the tongue—like kerplunckle and mollycoddle and pollywallydoodle. *Sandy.*"

"Sandy, darling, how did you get in here? Did Rupert let you in? Where is he?" Footsteps got dangerously close to the table, and Rupert closed his eyes.

"AH! Mrs. Campbell!" Witchling Two said, running toward the table, too. "Why don't we have some more of that tea again? Upstairs? Yes? Lovely? All right? Let's go!" Rupert heard sounds of shoe scuffling, and Rupert could see the shadows of his mother and Witchling Two inch even closer to where he was hiding.

"Why is there a cauldron on the table? And why are there—oh sweet cream cheese—*what* is in those jars? Are you and Rupert pretending to be witches?"

"What? Oh, yes!" Witchling Two said cheerfully. "*Exactly.* You caught us!"

"Well I don't think that's appropriate behavior," Mrs. Campbell said. "Those witches have nasty tempers, and . . ." Mrs. Campbell stood on her tiptoes, craning her neck. "Is that a shoe under the table? Rupert, are you there?"

Rupert cursed under his breath and rolled out from under the table. He emerged, hesitantly, afraid of what his mother might say about his new lima bean tan.

"Uh . . . Hi, Mom."

Mrs. Campbell screamed. Then her eyes rolled back in her head, and she fell to the floor with a thump.

"That was a lot easier than I thought it was going to be," Witchling Two said.

"Easier? You've killed her!" Rupert ran over to his mother—but thankfully she was breathing and had a pulse.

"It's the shock that does it," Witchling Two said. "I can't tell you how many people have had that reaction to me over the years."

"How many?" asked Rupert.

"I just said I couldn't tell you."

Rupert sighed. "We were so close."

"But so near."

"So far," Rupert corrected. He thought about how easily Witchling Two lied. "Sandy. Where did that come from?"

Witchling Two grinned. "Well, I wanted to wait for a ta-da moment, but I guess this will have to do." She stood on her tiptoes and thrust her chest outward. "I thought of my *name*. When I pass the Bar Exam. Sandy . . . it comes from . . . well . . ." she looked up at him with a sheepish blush. "I want to be the Sand Witch."

Rupert cracked open with laughter. "The *Sand* Witch?" he snickered. "Do you know how ridiculous that sounds?"

Witchling Two harrumphed. "Don't laugh! I thought it was a very respectable name. And it's so appropriate for me."

"You did give me a sand potion. And you thought of the idea of showering ourselves in sand to get away from Witchling Four. And you did make a sand dome to hide from the Council," Rupert agreed.

"I've given this a lot of thought, and you had better call me Sandy now," Witchling Two said, and Rupert knew her mind was made up.

Mrs. Campbell began to snore on the ground, and Sandy looked at her with pity. She walked over to Rupert's mother and began to hoist her by her left armpit, and Rupert grabbed her right one. They tried to drag her up the stairs, but she was too heavy. So instead they dragged her to the basement closet and rested her head on a mop. Rupert locked the door to the broom cupboard.

If his mother was passed out in a closet, the Fairfoul Witch might not see her. At least not for the moment.

"Sorry, Mom," he said, "but this is because I love you."

Sandy put her arm around him. "She really will be safest there, oh Green Machine with no Spleen who is Seen to Wean Clean Teens off Keen Beans—"

"About that," Rupert said. "You better get me to Storm and Nebby stat—unless you want me to choke you until you're purple."

Sandy squealed. "Purple is my favorite color!" she said, clapping her hands together. "And oh! That reminds me! Do you have any lollipops?"

The Nebulous Witch's Lair

SANDY AND RUPERT ESCAPED TO NEBBY'S LAIR once the sun had set. Sandy was able to shower them both in sand from a playground's sandbox, so they were safe from the Fairfoul Witch's watchful eyes.

Nebby's lair was the kind of house that Rupert's mother liked to look at in the real estate magazines—a very modern-looking place with lots of windows, mirrors, and strange-angled walls. It was very bright and clean looking. Quite the opposite of anything Rupert would expect of a witch's lair.

As soon as Rupert walked in the door, Nebby put up a pot of tea and disappeared into the kitchen to bake something. Rupert prayed it wouldn't be

Toecorn or Knuckle Soup, but when she emerged with a pan, it looked like perfectly harmless chocolate chunk cookies.

"Why are you being so nice to me?" Rupert asked, biting into a cookie. "I thought witches were mean and evil and horrid."

Sandy sniffled. "You didn't think that about me, did you, Greeny?"

"Stop calling me that!"

Nebby smiled. "Some witches *are* mean and evil and horrid, much like some humans are mean and evil and horrid. But like humans, not all witches are nasty. I personally don't enjoy harming things that don't harm me. And since I've raised Witchling Two, I've taught her my values."

Somewhere from the back of the house, Storm hooted, "NO, NEBBY! SHE LEARNED THEM FROM MEEEEEE!"

"Is she all right?" Rupert whispered to Sandy.

"Oh, yes," she said. "That's why she's called the Storm Witch, you know—because of her unpredictable outbursts of emotion."

Nebby put her hand on Rupert's arm. "You little green thing," she said. Then she frowned at Sandy, who plunked into a white armchair with her shoulders hunched.

In seconds, Nebby turned Rupert back to a pink thing, all traces of green now gone. Rupert sighed in relief, as he examined himself in a mirror. For a few horrible moments, he thought that he would look like freshly mowed grass forever.

"We don't feel comfortable sending you back home at night," Nebby said.

"But I have to get back to my mom," Rupert said. "We've locked her in a closet, and she's the only family I have."

"That's all good and kind," said Nebby. "But as soon as the Fairfoul Witch realizes how strongly you feel about your mother, she will use that to hurt you."

Rupert kicked the leg of the table. "Then what should I do?" he said, his face desperate. "How do I keep my mother safe *and* still be friends with Sandy? I still need to help her pass her Bar Exam—we only have four days left, and Sandy is in no shape to pass. And she still needs to help me with Mrs. Frabbleknacker, who tried to claw my eyes out when I left class today."

In all the excitement with the Fairfoul Witch, Rupert had almost forgotten that Mrs. Frabbleknacker was still livid with him. Compared to the problem of the Fairfoul Witch, facing Mrs. Frabbleknacker seemed like a breeze. But even if she was the last concern in his mind, she was still a niggling worry.

The Storm Witch coughed, and all eyes turned to her. "Bear warning at night and by the morning's light make right."

Nebby and Sandy nodded thoughtfully.

"Yes, that's exactly it," Nebby said, and she put a hand on Rupert's shoulder. "After Storm and I left your house, we did talk to a member of the Council of Three—someone quite close to the Fairfoul Witch—and she did not seem optimistic about your situation, Rupert. To be honest, you're in trouble. Much more trouble than you can even imagine."

"Because I belong to the witches, right?" he said accidentally.

"So . . . you and our witchling *were* snooping around the Witches Council lair." She winked. "Yes . . . you are claimed. It seems like both you and your mother are on thin ice with the witches."

"Why?" Rupert asked. "What happened with my mom?"

Nebby pursed her lips. "I'm not exactly sure, Rupert. This falls under the territory of the Fairfoul Witch. I only know what our records show—that your mother stole a forbidden potion, and the witches claimed you."

He sulked. "That's all I know, too."

"But it seems to me that you have two options. You can stay in Gliverstoll, in which case the Fairfoul Witch will most certainly find you. Or you can try to leave. In which case, you have a very, very small chance of success if—and only if—Storm and I can successfully distract the Fairfoul Witch."

"So . . . I should leave? But I've never left Gliverstoll before."

"You shall stay here tonight, and tomorrow we will send you to school like any normal boy. During the day, Storm and I will make sure that your school, neighborhood, and house are safe to return to—and double-check that the witches didn't lay out any traps for you or your mother. If there's a problem, one of us will find you at school. Otherwise, scurry home, quick as a lick, and then flee Gliverstoll with your mother. We'll distract the Fairfoul Witch and the entire Council while you make your escape. You'll need our help—otherwise, they'll know and drag you back in an instant."

"Why can't we do this *now*?" Rupert said impatiently.

"The Fairfoul Witch is out and about during these hours. If we head to your house, the Fairfoul Witch will learn of our betrayal. But the Fairfoul Witch sleeps during your school hours and wakes up at three-quarters to the witching hour."

"What's that?" Rupert said.

Sandy stroked her chin. "That's a human gibbon o'clock."

"Gibbon?"

"Erm . . . nine plus eight? What do you call that?

"Seventeen?"

"Yes!" Sandy said. "Seventeen o'clock."

"But what is *that?*" Rupert said, starting to lose his patience.

"Twenty-four hours in a day, seventeen hours past none o'clock."

Rupert scratched his head. "I don't understand witch math," he said.

"No matter," Nebby said. "After school, run right home. Then grab your mother and flee as fast as you can."

"If you don't cause any commotion, you'll be leopards of miles away before the Fairfoul Witch even brushes her teeth," Sandy said.

"But I can't go to school! Mrs. Frabbleknacker is mad beyond mad at me!"

Sandy gasped. "She *is?*"

"It's *your* fault, you know!"

"Oh."

Nebby shook her head. "I'm sorry, Rupert, but you must. If you deviate from what other kids are doing, you'll stick out to the other witches who are on the lookout for you. The only way to escape is to go to school and not to act suspiciously."

"But what do I do about Mrs. Frabbleknacker?"

"Mrs. Frickleknuckers is nothing compared to the Fairfoul Witch, Rupert," Sandy said. "You can face her."

"You must," Nebby said. "And then you must run away forever, Rupert," Nebby said. "You and your mother will only be safe if you never come back."

Rupert frowned. He didn't want to think it. But

he couldn't avoid the thought. "And what if . . ." Rupert said, letting the horrible thought come to his lips. "What if we don't escape the witches? What then?"

Storm ran a finger across her throat, miming the slit of a knife. She frowned and looked at him sadly, like he was already a goner.

The Last Class

IN THE MORNING, NEBBY, STORM, AND SANDY walked Rupert to the nearest bus stop. Sandy rubbed her eyes, trying to contain her tears. Storm did not have the same restraint—she sobbed and wiped her nose on the sleeve of her robes. Rupert was flattered that Storm felt so strongly about him—until she whispered, "That morning sun is so lovely!"

Rupert looked up at Nebby, who reached out a hand to help Rupert up.

"You must leave town—as quickly and quietly as you can," Nebby reminded him. "You and your mother should be safe once you get far enough away."

"And don't forget to mind your Z's and two's," Storm said.

"And don't worry about Mrs. Frabblecrackers," Sandy said. "The sand potion should still be in your system from yesterday, at least for a little while. I don't think she'll give you any trouble."

"Can I use the leftover potion in my water bottle?" Rupert asked.

Sandy shook her head. "That should be stale. We could have made a new one, but . . ." Sandy whimpered. And that whimper turned into a snivel. And that snivel turned into a weep. And that weep turned into a cry. And that cry turned into a wail. And that wail turned into a sob. And that sob turned into a blubber.

"I'm sorry!" Sandy said, wiping her face on her arm. "I know I'm only supposed to cry when I'm happy! But you were the best friend I ever had!"

Watching her, Rupert was gutted. "Me too," he said miserably. He tried to memorize her round face, her freckles, her blond hair tucked in a high ponytail, her big teeth—he couldn't believe that this was the last time he would ever see Sandy.

"Do well on your Bar Exam," Rupert said. "You only have three days left, so you better practice a lot."

"I will," Sandy sniffled.

Rupert nodded. "You'll be the best Sand Witch anyone has ever seen."

They hugged, and the emptiness grew inside his chest.

The bus came, and Rupert went to the very last row so he could wave to Sandy as the bus drove him to the worst place in the world. At first Sandy waved back, but then they grew farther and farther apart, until she was just a speck in his field of vision—and then she was gone altogether.

Rupert turned around, crossed his arms, and scowled. *Just* when he found a friend that Mrs. Frabbleknacker couldn't take away, he still couldn't be friends with her, all because of another horrible adult—the Fairfoul Witch. The more he thought about it, the more steamed he became. Who was Mrs. Frabbleknacker to stop him from talking to his friends? And who was the Fairfoul Witch to make him leave town?

When the school bus finally arrived, Rupert shuffled into the hallway, walked into his classroom, and took his seat. A few jaws dropped when he walked in, and poor brave Bruno leaned over and whispered, "We thought you were a goner."

Rupert shrugged. He hurt in the bottom of his chest, in the pit of his stomach. He wanted to cry.

But he put on a brave smile and said to Bruno, "Nope, I'm just fine."

"What did Mrs. Frabbleknacker do?" Allison asked. "Did she pull your hair?"

"Did she stomp on your toes?" said Kaleigh.

"Did she poke you in the side with a spoon?" said Hal.

"Did she sock you in the stomach?" squeaked Manny, from his little glass jar on the windowsill.

"She didn't do anything," he said. And he sat down in his seat, very aware that the rest of the class was staring at him with awe.

Not a moment later, the door burst open, and Mrs. Frabbleknacker blew in. She sniffed and looked around the room very carefully. Her eyes stopped when she reached Rupert's desk, but Rupert noticed that she squinted slightly as she stared at him, as if he was blurry and she couldn't quite see him.

"Children," she said, as though she was saying something truly awful like *Ingrown Toenail* or *Hairy Ice Cream*. "Today is for mathematics."

Everyone groaned.

"Hush!" Mrs. Frabbleknacker said, crinkling her criggly nose. "Now I know you may be disappointed. I know you thought that because we hadn't done mathematics thus far, we weren't going to do it ever. But you were wrong. You're always wrong. If you are always wrong and never right, then what percentage are you wrong?"

"One hundred percent," the class droned.

"WRONG!" Mrs. Frabbleknacker jumped up. "You are wrong hyrax percent!"

Rupert scratched his head and wrote *hyrax = 100* in his notebook.

Mrs. Frabbleknacker walked to the front of the classroom, her heels clicking. She stopped when she got to the jar that trapped Manny. She stared at him. "If I say that Manny is two plus three inches tall, then how tall is he?" Mrs. Frabbleknacker whipped around, her eyes bulging. "Allison!"

"F-five?"

Mrs. Frabbleknacker jumped in the air and pointed at Allison. "FIVE? FIVE?" Mrs. Frabbleknacker walked over to Allison. The whole class cringed. Rupert stood very still, his stomach sinking. Surely, Allison was in for it now.

Mrs. Frabbleknacker's face broke into a smile. A very waxy, cold-looking smile, as though she didn't quite know how to upturn her lips.

"Did you hear that, class?" Mrs. Frabbleknacker said. "Two plus three equals *five!* Well done, my dear Allison! Well done!"

She held out her hand for Allison to shake. Allison awkwardly held her own limp hand out to Mrs. Frabbleknacker. But instead of shaking Allison's hand, Mrs. Frabbleknacker yanked her out of her desk.

"WRONG!" Mrs. Frabbleknacker shouted. "TWO PLUS THREE IS *NOT* FIVE!"

She pulled both of Allison's arms over her head and tied them in a pretzel knot. Allison squeaked. Then she ran from the classroom crying, yet again.

Mrs. Frabbleknacker walked to the front of the classroom. "Now who can tell me what two plus three is? Anyone?"

The whole class was silent.

Mrs. Frabbleknacker stamped her foot on the ground. "IF YOU CAN'T ANSWER THIS SIMPLE QUESTION," she shouted, "THEN HOW ARE YOU GOING TO LEARN HARD MATH? HOW

WILL YOU BE ABLE TO ANSWER JACKAL
DIVIDED BY BELUGA? OR PARAKEET MULTI-
PLIED BY CAMEL?"

Rupert's heart stopped, and his head grew light
and dizzy. Jackal? Beluga? Parakeet? Camel? And . . .
Hyrax? No wonder he didn't know that *hyrax = 100*.
Hyrax wasn't a word for one hundred—hyrax was
an animal. And if Mrs. Frabbleknacker expected
them to multiply and divide with animals, it could
only mean one thing.

"Now we'll try this again," Mrs. Frabbleknacker
said. "Two plus three is—"

"Honeybee," said Rupert.

He locked eyes with Mrs. Frabbleknacker, and
she grinned.

The Worst
Witch of All

THE WHOLE CLASS LOOKED AT RUPERT. BUT
Rupert didn't have time to worry about them. His
thoughts buzzed and hummed and flung around like
Silly Putty in a slingshot. Every witch-like moment
that had made him suspicious about her suddenly
rushed back to him, and all the pieces made perfect sense. The cruel punishments—that was very
witch-like behavior. The animal math—that was
witch math. Mrs. Frabbleknacker didn't *buy* her
potions—she made them. Probably with the frog
guts that she got from his class. She didn't even
hate the witches—she must have been pretending

because she didn't want anyone to know that she *was* a witch. This whole time.

Mrs. Frabbleknacker turned her back toward Rupert and scratched the chalkboard with a ruler. The sound made Rupert shudder, and when she stepped away from the board, Rupert read:

LIFE IS FAIR, AND FAIR IS FOUL.

Rupert's mouth went dry. Warning words fired in his brain. Fair. Foul. Fairfoul. Fairfoul Witch. Not only was Mrs. Frabbleknacker a witch, but she was the *Fairfoul* Witch, the only witch that made Nebby, Storm, and Sandy quake in their boots.

Rupert's eyes darted for the door. He had to get out.

Mrs. Frabbleknacker—or the Fairfoul Witch— drifted dangerously close to Rupert's only escape, as if she read his eye movements. Rupert weighed his options. He could make a break for the window, or he could distract her as he dashed for the door. But deep down, he knew that neither of these would work. The Fairfoul Witch had powerful and unlimited magic on her side, and Rupert only had the sand potion in his veins, which was just about expired.

Rupert wondered if the Fairfoul Witch would

really hurt him in front of the rest of the class. That would be a liability, right? She would get fired. She could go to jail.

Who was he kidding? The Fairfoul Witch didn't care about that stuff. She could use her magic to escape—and who would believe the fifth-grade witnesses anyway?

Rupert felt sick—nauseous in the pit of his stomach, clammy sweat on his neck. The Fairfoul Witch had him trapped and cornered.

He was dead meat.

He looked up at the Fairfoul Witch again, and she seemed to be watching him with upturned lips and a twinkle in her eye. Rupert forced himself to calm down—he focused on his breathing. In and out. Inhale and exhale. The more he focused on his breathing, the calmer he got, and the more disinterested the Fairfoul Witch became.

She turned back to the board with a click of her heels and pointed to her clawed message on the chalkboard: *LIFE IS FAIR, AND FAIR IS FOUL.*

"This is our new class motto," the Fairfoul Witch said. "Repeat."

"Life is fair. And fair is foul," the class droned.

"Louder!'

"LIFE IS FAIR, AND FAIR IS FOUL."

The Fairfoul Witch sniffed, her grandflubbing nose twitching. "Today's lesson is about a little boy. A little boy who broke the rules. A little boy who spends his afternoons gallivanting with a witchling. A little boy who tried to trick me." She licked her lips. "Tell me, class, what should I do with a little boy like that?"

No one said anything.

"Today's lesson," the Fairfoul Witch continued, "is one that will be important for the rest of your lives. The first part is that life is fair. A little boy disobeys and sneaks?—well, he gets his proper punishment. The second part is that fair is foul." She smiled, revealing a mouth of crooked teeth. "Punishment is not pleasant. Punishment for bad actions—though fair—is often foul. Tragic," she said, as if she was already anticipating newspaper headlines. She loomed close to Rupert, her clawed hands outstretched like she was ready to strangle him.

Rupert dug into his backpack for something— anything—to stop the Fairfoul Witch. His fingers grazed books, pens, notebooks—his hand closed around his water bottle of sand potion. It wouldn't work—Sandy said it was stale. He quickly undid the cap anyway.

The Fairfoul Witch loomed over him. "You're finished!" she crowed.

Rupert took the potion out of his bag and splashed the Fairfoul Witch in the face. She howled and hissed as if her eyes sizzled. "AUGHHHHHHHHH! POTION IN MY EYES!"

Rupert dropped his backpack, ducked around her, and made for the door. His sweaty palms clasped around the doorknob—he turned the knob and kicked the door open. Outside the classroom door were nine women and four girls in black cloaks. Rupert recognized Witchling Four, the Storm Witch, and the Nebulous Witch among them. The other women, he assumed, must be the rest of the Witches Council. And the girls must be the other witchlings.

"Nebby! Storm! Please! My teacher Mrs. Frabbleknacker is the Fairfoul Witch! Help!"

But Nebby just leered at him. Storm began to

cackle, and soon all of the witches were tittering, snorting, crowing, and guffawing.

He could feel his face getting hot with rage—how could he be so *stupid*?

This time, thought Rupert, *there really is no escape.*

The Potion! The Potion!

As the witches inched closer and closer, the taste in his mouth soured. He had dropped his backpack before running out of the classroom—the only weapon he had was himself. He lifted his hands in a boxing position, ready to sock the first witch that laid a hand on him.

The witches cackled.

"Vhat's zat, boy?" one witch said. This witch was taller than all the others. She had short tangled black hair, a sharp pointy face, small lips, a tiny flat nose, and angry-looking eyes clouded by dark circles. "Vere you going to vhack me vith your fists?"

"If I have to," Rupert said. "Stay away!"

The witches howled and snorted.

"I am ze Zunder Vitch," she laughed. "I vill not be vorried by a little boy."

"Zunder Vitch?" Rupert said. *Oh! Thunder Witch!* he realized.

"Let me at 'im!" shouted a hoarse voice. "I'll smack 'em with a dead fish!"

The witches stepped even closer—so close that they were only a stride away. He had to think, and think fast. He closed his eyes for a second, trying to remember what Sandy had told him about the Witches Council. There was the head witch—the Fairfoul Witch. And then there was an underdog . . . no, an Undercat—the Midnight Witch. What had Sandy said about her? She was just as frightening as the Fairfoul Witch—and she was also dying to over-throw the head witch. *This can help,* Rupert thought.

"WAIT!" Rupert shouted. "W-which one of you is the Midnight Witch?"

The witches stopped in their tracks, but no one answered him. He scanned their faces for a moment, and his gaze finally rested on a plump woman with skin so white that she looked green. Her eyes were sunken, and she had warts all over.

"You dare speak my name?" she said, in a voice so quiet that it sent chills through Rupert.

"You're the Undercat," he said. "If you can help me overthrow the Fairfoul Witch—*you* could be the head witch!"

The Midnight Witch growled. "I do not *team up* with *humanssssss*," she hissed. She ran her tongue across her front teeth and snarled:

RANK RANCID ROT
STALE SOUR STINK
FOUL FETID FILTH
BAD BRAINLESS BOY
DEEPLY DEFILES
WAYS OF THE WITCH.

Her long, fat fingers grabbed Rupert's arm, and she dug her sharp nails into his flesh. Rupert tried to wriggle free, but other witches began to grab him, pinning him against the lockers. The Nebulous Witch stood in his line of sight, and he scowled at her—she ran a hand through his hair, holding his head back and tilted upward.

"The potion!" the witches said. "The potion!"

With one free hand, the Nebulous Witch reached into her cloak and pulled out a purple vial. She clicked open the top, and a bit of smoke clouded the air. It smelled like musty rain on a summer's day. Rupert coughed.

The Nebulous Witch leaned close to Rupert.

"I thought I could trust you!" Rupert said.

"Your mistake," the Nebulous Witch said. "Poor little Witchling Two—she's all alone on Main Beach, so sad about your departure."

"Are you going to tell her what really happened?" Rupert said. "How you betrayed me and fed me to the witches? How you poisoned me with your potion?"

"If that's the story you want her to hear, I'll tell her." The Nebulous Witch smirked, and there was an evil gleam in her eyes. "Bottoms up, Rupert."

She tipped the potion to his lips. Rupert tried to keep his mouth sealed tight. He closed his eyes and scrunched his face. The juice dripped down his cheeks, into his ears—until something sharp rapped him on the jaw, and he opened his mouth in pain.

The syrupy potion glopped into his mouth, and before he could stop himself, he swallowed.

Unexpected Effects

RUPERT FELT THE POTION SLIDE ALL THE WAY down. For a moment, he felt nothing but the cold fear that coursed through him. The witches were still holding him against the locker, and he tried to imagine himself somewhere else. He didn't want his last moment to be this. More than anything, he wanted to find his mother and apologize—she was right about the witches all along. Except for *his* witchling, they weren't to be trusted.

I'm sorry, Mom, he thought. *And I'm sorry, Sandy—I wish we could have been friends without all this mess.*

Rupert closed his eyes and let a tear escape. He concentrated on his breathing—in and out, inhale and exhale—until he felt calm and warmth spreading from the pit of his stomach out to his limbs.

Then he twitched.

He opened his eyes, and realized his legs were dangling. Suddenly he fell to the floor and curled up. His cheeks trembled, and out of his peripheral vision he saw four long and stiff white hairs protruding from each side of his face. He hopped forward and saw his reflection in the mirror.

He was a rabbit.

His ears flung backward, and he scratched his face with his paws.

He looked up at the witches, but they were all looking at their hands as if they had just touched poison ivy.

"Vhat's zis?" the Thunder Witch shrieked. "Ze potion vas not supposed to turn zis boy into a rabbit!"

Rupert hopped away from them, but they all chased him. Rupert cowered against a locker, and shuddered.

POP! he heard. *POP! POP! POP! POP! POP! POP! POP! POP! POP! POP! POP! POP!*

He turned around to see thirteen fluffy rabbits on the floor with him, all hopping around in panic.

"It vas ze potion!" a ginger bunny shrieked. It

sounded an awful lot like the Thunder Witch, but with a much higher, squeakier voice. "Ze potion is an Untouchable!"

"We were holding onto the boy! We touched him, and he has spread the potion!" a black bunny yelped, and all the witch-bunnies hopped around in panic.

The closest classroom door opened, and the Fairfoul Witch burst into the hallway. "Well?" she said. "Is he dead?"

The thirteen witch rabbits jumped onto the Fairfoul Witch's feet, and she screamed. A moment later, Rupert heard a *POP*, and the Fairfoul Witch turned into a rabbit.

The rabbit-witches leaped into Rupert's class, and Rupert heard cries of delight from his classmates, who all swooped down to pet the fuzzy bunnies. Moments later, Rupert heard more *POP*s, and he peeked his head in the classroom to see twenty-six new bunnies hopping around—and no children.

Rupert backed away from the classroom. What was going on? He thought he was going to die, but instead he became a fluffy bunny. And so did the witches. And so did the kids in his class.

Rupert heard a tiny squeak from behind him. "Go!" a brown bunny said. "You know where! And don't touch anyone—or else they'll turn into rabbits, too!" Then the brown bunny disappeared back into the classroom.

Rupert hopped and hopped and hopped—out of his school, across the street, and down the stairs that led to Main Beach. He had never hopped so much in his life, and his little bunny heart beat wildly. At the bottom of the stairs, he stopped to catch his breath. Then he hopped forward with renewed vigor.

When he reached the sand, Rupert found that it was much harder to hop. The sand slid underneath him, and it required twice as much energy to jump. Up in the distance, he saw a girl with blond hair tucked under a wide-brimmed hat standing with her pants rolled up, her calves in the ocean. She was the only one on the beach, and even from far away, Rupert knew it was Sandy.

He pushed himself to go farther and faster—he needed to get to her before the bunnies overtook the entire town. After much more hopping, he was right behind her, watching her hair sway in the wind.

He cleared his throat. "Sand Witch!" he squeaked. "It's me!"

Sandy turned around and stared at his rabbit form. She blinked for a moment. "BUUUNNNYY-YYYYYYYYYY! AAAAAAAAHHHHHHHHHHH-HHHHHHHHHHH!"

"No! No!" Rupert shouted. "It's me! Rupert!"

"TALKING BUNNY! TALKING LYING BUNNY!" She took off her shoe and threw it at Rupert, and Rupert jumped to the side to avoid it.

"I'm not lying! It's Rupert! Really! The Fairfoul Witch caught me! The Witches Council gave me a potion that turned me into this!"

Sandy froze in horror, a nauseated expression on her face.

"You have to help me," Rupert said. "The witches are chasing me! Well, they're not really witches anymore—they've all turned into bunnies."

She blanched. "They've all turned into bunnies?" Sandy said with a shudder. "That's the only thing worse than witches!"

"But it's not just the witches—everyone in my class has turned into bunnies, too. And anyone who touches us becomes a bunny—soon the whole town will be full of bunnies!"

Sandy winced. "What can I do?"

"You have to turn us back!"

She shook her head. "I can't. My spells are still rubbish, remember?"

"I'll help you," Rupert said. "I'll coach you through it. You're the only witch that can stop it. All the other witches and witchlings are rabbits right now. Without you, Gliverstoll is doomed."

Sandy held her arms close to her chest and trembled again. "I. HATE. RABBITS," she said through clenched teeth. "We certainly can't have a town full of them."

"If enough people turn into them, you might become one, too," Rupert said. "I imagine it would be hard to fight off a horde of bunnies."

Sandy shuddered violently. "Please stop talking about them! Just . . . let me think of an appropriate spell."

She sat down on the sand across from Rupert and buried her face in her hands. Rupert waited patiently as she mumbled. "Honey," she said. "And money. And funny—oh, that's no good. Rabbit—habit. Still no good. What about people? Oh . . . steeple."

"What are you doing?" Rupert asked.

Sandy looked up. "Trying to think of all the ways my spell can go wrong."

Rupert's nose twitched, and he stuck his bunny ears straight up. "We'll be here forever, if you do that," he said.

Sandy sighed. Then she froze, staring at something behind Rupert. He turned his head—thousands of bunnies were hopping down the steps. Black ones, white ones, gray ones, brown ones, tan ones, dotted ones, plain ones. They were pouring down like water out of a watering can, showering down the stairs. From a distance, Rupert thought the bunnies made the steps look like they were covered with a shaggy rug.

Sandy's bottom lip quivered. "BUUUUNNN-NNYYYYYYYYYYYYYYYYYYY! AAAAAAAAH-HHHHHHHHHHHHHHHHHHHHHHH!"

"GO!" Rupert squeaked. "YOU CAN'T TOUCH THEM! YOU HAVE TO GET OUT OF HERE!"

Sandy started to run, but then she hesitated. "You're coming with me," she said. "Rupert Rabbit, you had better be fast!"

A Brief Interlude from Real Bunnies

To Whom it May Concern:

We're not that scary.

We're actually pretty fluffy, warm, and snuggly-wuggly soft.

Okay. Sure, some of us carry nasty little diseases. And sure, the Black Plague rode in on our distant cousins— the rodents—but that wasn't *our* fault. And we formally protest our horrible reputation. Consider this letter

our formal complaint regarding our
cruel repute. We are certain that you
will take the appropriate measures
to ensure that our reputation as a
lovable animal will be restored.

                            Cordially,
        Common Association of Rampant Rabbits
            for the Order and Triumph of Society
(CARROTS)

All the Ways a Spell Can Go Wrong

RUPERT HOPPED. AND HOPPED. AND HOPPED.
He hopped as fast as his bunny legs could drudge through the sand. Sandy stood next to him and cheered him on, but the flock of bunnies behind them was moving too fast for poor, tired Rupert.

"You've got to keep going without me," Rupert panted.

Sandy cringed and laid her hat on the ground. "Hop in," she said.

Rupert jumped into her hat, and she folded it around him, just to make sure that he wouldn't accidentally touch her. She whispered into the hat, "Hold on, Rupert Rabbit!" and then she ran

219

as fast as her little witchy legs could take her.

Rupert jostled around in the hat, feeling very disconcerted and dizzy and frazzled. *If this is what animals feel like when they're picked up by humans, I'm never touching another one again,* he thought.

Finally, the bumpy run stopped, and the next thing Rupert knew, he was being tousled out of the hat. He fell splat onto a table, where he lay with all four legs sprawled out while Sandy locked the door.

He recognized the room. They were in Sandy's lair in Pexale Close—where Rupert had first met Sandy during his interview. He hadn't been there for a long while, since the witches booby-trapped it with their magic, but it looked the same as it did before. It was still musty and smelly, like the sole of a sweaty shoe, and knickknacks were still all over the shelves. The only thing that looked different was that there were loads of spiderwebs everywhere.

"Are we safe here?" Rupert said.

Sandy nodded. "For now." Sandy walked to her supply cabinet and pulled a piece of wilted lettuce out of the fridge. She set the lettuce in front of Rupert, and then she sat down on a stool.

Rupert jumped forward and began to nibble at the greens.

"What am I going to do, Rupert?" Sandy suddenly cried. "I'm not a good enough witch to save anybody in the town, let alone everybody!"

"I know you can do it," Rupert said with his mouth full of lettuce. "And Nebby and Storm believe in you, too."

Sandy peeked at Rupert through her fingers.

"What are you doing?" Rupert asked.

"I can't look at you," she shuddered. "Those ears! That tail! That twitchy nose!"

Rupert hopped behind a stack of books. "I'm hidden so you don't have to look at me anymore. Just listen to my voice—I'll coach you through this."

"Okay!" Sandy said. "What do I do, Rupert?"

Rupert poked his head above the books so that he could catch a secret glance at Sandy, but she screamed.

"DON'T. DO. THAT," she said. "GO AWAY AGAIN!"

Rupert ducked back down.

Sandy cleared her throat. "I need to think of how to phrase my words so that they won't mess up. But the only words I can think of that don't sound like anything else are *orange, silver,* and *month,* but I don't see how any of those relate to the spell I need."

"No," Rupert agreed, "they don't."

Just then, scratching sounds came from the door. Rupert knew the noises came from a boatload of bunnies trying to get in. He looked at Sandy in panic, and she collapsed on the table. "There *have* to be more words that don't rhyme!"

Rupert gasped. "That's it!" he said, turning his head to look at the door. The scratches were growing increasingly louder, and he knew that they only had about another minute before the bunnies clawed their way through the wooden door. "Maybe we're going about this backward!"

"How?"

"Instead of trying to think of words that don't sound like anything else, we need to think of words that *do* sound like the words we want. Get it?"

Sandy shook her head no. "Not really."

Rupert urgently thumped his foot on the table. "Your spell casting is opposite, so you need to approach it backwardly. So let's say you wanted to turn me invisible. Instead of saying *can't be seen* you say *turning green*. Then maybe the opposite of your intended spell will happen and I really would turn invisible."

Sandy clapped. "Rupert, you're brilliant! Thank goodness I asked for a smart apprentice!"

Splintering sounds came from the door, and Rupert saw a tiny rabbit nail break through. *Help us!* the rabbits cried. *Help us!*

"STAY BACK!" Rupert shouted. Then he turned to Sandy. "Test it on me. That way if things go wrong, you won't have messed up on an entire town."

Sandy gulped. "Um . . . see a toy!" she snapped her fingers.

Rupert felt a tingling sensation all throughout his body. His fur fell off his body, landing at his bald bunny feet like a new carpet. Then his arms and legs expanded, stretching out like taffy until they hung slack at his sides. With a whoosh, clothes materialized over his loose limbs. His eyes rolled back into his head and came back white and brown, rather than like black coals. Hair sprouted out of his head. And with a final *POP,* his ears shrunk and his nose wiggled back to its normal size.

Rupert stumbled to a mirror—he was himself again!

"See a toy?" he said to Sandy.

"Be a boy! It was all I could think of!"

The wood on the door splintered again, this time big enough for a bunny to hop through. A black bunny with milky eyes soared through the hole in the door and hopped toward Sandy. *Help us!* the bunny said. A group of bunnies followed in the black bunny's wake. Rupert supposed there were fifty of them in total.

Sandy shivered and backed into a shelf. "Stay away," she said. "I'll help you if you stay away."

The bunnies hopped closer, and Rupert swung his legs onto the table to avoid them.

"Hurry!" he said. "I can't help you if you get turned into a rabbit!"

Sandy closed her eyes and snapped her fingers. "Attack in two steeples! Attack in two steeples! ATTACK IN TWO STEEPLES! AUGHHHHHHH!" she shouted as the bunnies jumped toward her.

Sandy whimpered and wailed—but in mid-leap, the fifty bunnies shed their hair, sprouted arms and legs, and lost their ears. Fifty people stood in Sandy's small lair, packed so tightly that no one could move an elbow.

Sandy snapped. "Wet snout!"

The door sprung open, and everyone scrambled for the exit. Except for Rupert.

He turned to the panting witch with a grin. "Get out," he said. "Nice touch!"

Sandy ran over and hugged him. And it was the best hug ever.

What To Do
About the Witches

"BUT WAIT," RUPERT SAID, BREAKING AWAY FROM Sandy's hug. "Where are the witches? Are they still coming to find me?"

Sandy burst out in giggles. "That's the best part!" she said. She ran outside, and Rupert followed her. They walked around town for what seemed like forever, but as soon as Sandy led him past the fish-and-chips restaurant, Rupert knew exactly where they were headed—to the witches' lair. They walked up to the boulder that marked the entrance, and Sandy put her hand on the rock, which grumbled and rolled to the side to reveal the passageway into the heart of the lair. And there, in the entrance to the lair, fourteen bunnies huddled together.

Sandy cringed at the sight of the bunnies, but she quickly snapped her fingers and conjured a cage that surrounded all the bunnies. Then she held her hands out in a ta-da pose.

"What's that for?" Rupert said.

"The Witches Council!" Sandy laughed. "And four witchlings."

Rupert's mouth fell agape. "But how?"

"Attack in two steeples," Sandy said. "Turn back into people. But the witches were never people—they were always witches. It was a tiny loophole that I thought might work."

Rupert stared at the bunnies. A gray one bared its teeth, while the rest looked humbled and frightened.

"Turn us back!" the gray one squealed. "By order of the Fairfoul Witch, I command you!"

"The Fairfoul Witch, huh?" said Rupert. He picked up a nearby stick and poked the Fairfoul Witch gently in the side. She hissed and tried to bite the stick, but Rupert poked her again.

Sandy stroked her chin with her thumb and pointer. "Weelllllll," she said. "Look at this. I'm the only one who has the power to change the bunnies back into witches."

"Oh please, please!" squeaked a few spotted bunnies.

Rupert scanned the bunnies and found the brown bunny that he recognized as Nebby—she was hanging back behind the group with a tawny-looking bunny, which Rupert assumed was Storm. Both their whiskers twitched, but they did not say a peep.

"Hmmm . . ." Sandy said. "I should turn them all back into witches. They are my family after all, and we witches *do* do a lot of secret things that keep Gliverstoll working." Sandy paced around. "But *will* I?"

Sandy winked at Rupert, who took his cue. "I don't know," he said. "I sure would hate to have to lick their feet or eat my way out of a pool full of Jell-O."

The Fairfoul Bunny snarled a deep throaty snarl, but the other bunny witches began to plead. "Oh please!" they said. "Please, Witchling Two, turn us back! We will leave the boy alone! Just turn us back!"

"I demand to be materialized back into my original form!" the Fairfoul Bunny said. "If you don't obey right now, I can assure you that you'll never be part of the Witches Council!"

Sandy folded her arms. "Then I can assure you that you'll all be bunnies forever."

"Please!" the rest of the witch-bunnies cried. "Turn us back!"

"Only if you promise to leave Rupert and his family alone," Sandy said.

"We promise! We promise!"

"I need written proof." Sandy whipped up a scroll and an inkpad with a snap, and each bunny pressed her paw into the inkpad and then marked the scroll.

The Fairfoul Bunny trudged over to the inkpad. "He broke the rules. You broke the rules. I will *not* agree to keeping him safe! He knows too much! He must perish—I shall make him eat the sludge from a fish tank—or I shall make him suck eggs up his nose with a straw—"

"No!" Sandy said. "I won't change any of you back until you all agree to leave him alone."

"But he is a human! We hate humans! We punish humans!" the Fairfoul Bunny howled.

"You may hate humans, but I don't," Sandy said. "And human or not, Rupert is my best friend, and I can't have you hurting him."

The Fairfoul Bunny dipped her paw into the inkpad. She glared at Sandy with her red eyes, and then she stamped the scroll, just below the signatures of the other bunny witches. "I will find some way around this," the Fairfoul Bunny said. "You mark my words—I will make this boy's life miserable!"

Rupert stared down at the Fairfoul Bunny. "You've made my whole year miserable," he said, "but from this point on, *you're* going to be miserable, not me. Isn't this what you call *fair* and *foul*?"

The Fairfoul Bunny spat. "How dare you speak to me like that! I will make you suffer in ways you can't even imagine. I can make your *mother* suffer."

Rupert trembled with anger. "What happened between you and my mother?"

"You mean you don't know?"

"I know my mom stole some forbidden potions from the witches, and you claimed me as punishment—"

"Told you!" squeaked a tiny ginger rabbit. "Told you Witchling Two brought him to see the files!"

"What did my mom steal?"

"A fertility potion," the Fairfoul Bunny snarled. "She wanted a baby."

Rupert sat down on the grass. "You—you mean—"

"Yes, you owe your entire existence to the witches, boy." She hopped forward, her red eyes glinting with glee. "But it's time to take back what was originally ours."

"And what's that then?" asked Rupert.

"You."

The Unfair Bargain

SANDY STEPPED IN FRONT OF RUPERT protectively, even though the bunnies were still stuck in their cage.

Rupert stepped out from behind her. "I don't belong to you! You can't take me!"

The Fairfoul Bunny lifted her upper lip and showed her enormous bunny teeth. "Oh, but I can. Your mother's punishment for stealing our forbidden potion was that we were allowed to take back the effects of the potion—you—at any time we wanted. Of course, that deal has since been amended . . ."

"What do you mean?" Rupert asked.

"Your pesky mother grew frightened and para- noid that we would claim you, and eventually, she tried to run away with you, but we dragged her back to Gliverstoll. She begged and pleaded for your freedom and your life, and eventually we came to . . . an agreement. I promised to leave you alone . . . in exchange for her services. For years, she has been serving me, doing all sorts of jobs—"

"*What* sort of jobs?" Rupert asked.

"Anything, everything—from delivering potions to our buyers, to testing any new potions, to scrubbing the floors of our lair. She has been paying for you with her labor, sweat, and tears." The Fairfoul Bunny laughed, and a few others chimed in—but some of the bunnies shook their heads, looking thoroughly unamused.

"My mom was right about you—you truly are horrible."

The Fairfoul Bunny bared her teeth and paced around the cage. "I didn't tell you the best part, yet. The deal with your mom stated that she was never allowed to leave Gliverstoll again, she was never to cross the witches, and . . ."

"And?"

"*You* were never to cross the witches."

That was why his mother never wanted him near

any witches. That was why she was always so over-protective.

"But now you have crossed the witches, the deal is broken, and you belong to me," she squealed. "And *believe* me when I say that I will make you pay, you foul, appalling child. You repugnant, wretched huma—"

"That's enough out of you," Sandy said coldly. "You can't touch Rupert or his family. And no threat you say matters anymore—you already signed the pledge, and now you have to leave Rupert and his family alone. Fairfoul Witch, I will hold you to your oath. I will hold you all to it. Now, I suppose I should honor my side of the agreement, too. I'll start with my guardians. Warm. Webby." Sandy snapped her fingers, and Storm and Nebby transformed from the tawny rabbit and the brown rabbit back into witches. Then they transfigured themselves out of the cage.

Sandy handed the contract to Nebby. "Can you put a magical seal on this? I want an expert to do it."

Nebby smiled. "Let's do it together."

Storm nodded. "All three of us. As a family."

They stood together, smiling. Then they each

snapped. Nebby and Storm said *seal*, but Rupert swore he heard Sandy say *peel*.

The scroll shimmered and rolled up, and Sandy grabbed it out of the air and handed it to Rupert. "Keep this safe," she said.

"And now for the Witches Council," Nebby said.

"Do you *have* to turn them back into witches?" Rupert said. "I think they're much more pleasant this way."

"You know I can't do that, Rupert."

Sandy put her arm around Rupert. "Let's just hope that the lot of them have learned their lessons!"

Nebby and Storm opened the cage and turned the witches back into their original forms. The Fairfoul Witch scowled, turned on her heel, and sulked into the cave. The Midnight Witch glared at Nebby. "Was this *your* doing?" she said.

"I don't know what you're talking about," said Nebby coolly. "I gave Rupert the same potion that was handed to me. If you wish to go around pointing fingers at other witches, then go ahead. But the last time our Council fell into chaos was also the time our last Undercat was overthrown. Just remember that."

The Midnight Witch stomped back into the

witches' lair. The rest of the Witches Council and the young witchlings followed suit.

Nebby put a hand on Rupert's shoulder. "We should get back to your mother," she said.

Storm's eyes bulged, but her lips cracked into a smile. "In the closet holds a mummy, for her it must be very crummy!"

"Storm," Sandy said. "You sure are good at rhyming words. I should pick your brain later about spells I could use."

Storm looked aghast and ran down the hill and across the street, shouting, "STAY AWAY FROM MY BRAIN!"

Rupert turned to Nebby. "Did you know about Mrs. Frabbleknacker the whole time?"

"The Witches Council just found out this morning. The Fairfoul Witch had us believe that she slept during the sunlight hours. Really, I don't know how she managed to conceal her job as a fifth-grade teacher for all this time. She truly is as good at magic as her title suggests."

"Fairfoul?"

"No, head witch."

"Oh," Rupert said. "You know, when you gave me that potion, I really thought you were trying to kill me!"

"I had to put on a show, Rupert," she said. "I still need to remain on the Council, but that doesn't mean I don't have a few tricks up my sleeve. I switched the vial of potion—I gave you something of my own concoction."

"Mmm, what was the potion?" Sandy asked. "I've never seen anything like that before!"

Nebby smiled. "It was a potion that turns the drinker—and whoever the drinker touches—into a rabbit. It's a highly contagious effect, which is exactly what the situation required—I knew that all the witches needed to be momentarily incapacitated, and I knew that my witchling would never touch a rabbit."

Sandy shook her head. "Nuh-uh. Not *ever*!"

Rupert scrunched his face in thought. "But didn't the other witches have magic, too? Couldn't they have stopped it?"

"Never underestimate the power of surprise, Rupert," said Nebby. "I caught them all off guard."

"BEAUTIFUL!" Storm shrieked, and from a distance, Rupert could see her skipping through flowers.

"That's my cue," said Nebby, and she followed Storm down the hill to calm her down.

Rupert and Sandy walked down the hill together, behind Sandy's family, toward Rupert's house.

Sandy kept bursting out in laughs, and soon she began to jump up and down. She grabbed Rupert's hand and pumped it up and down. "Rupert! Rupert, Rupert! Now we don't have to hide anymore! We can go on the playground and we can go get a milkshake and we can even go swimming! I'm so happy!" she said with a sniffle. "R-rupert? Can I cry now?"

"Knock yourself out," he said, and Sandy began to bawl on his shoulder as they walked down the street toward home.

Finally, the Truth: or, The End of an Era

RUPERT WALKED INTO HIS HOUSE WITH THE STORM Witch, the Nebulous Witch, and Sandy by his side. He instantly ran into the basement, where he could hear faint knocks from inside of the closet.

When Rupert opened the door, his mom stumbled out helplessly, falling to her knees. Her hair was all knotted, and dark circles surrounded her bloodshot eyes. At the sight of Rupert, she began to cry.

"Mom!" Rupert said. "I'm so sorr—"

But he didn't even have a chance to finish his sentence before his mother pulled him into a hug. She sobbed, kissing the top of his head over and over. Then she held him at arm's length and said,

"RUPERT ARCHIBALD CAMPBELL, IF YOU *EVER* DO ANYTHING LIKE THAT AGAIN . . ." But the next moment she folded him into her weeping, kissing embrace again.

Finally, his mother calmed down enough to sputter, "You are so grounded. Where in the world have you been?" She looked up, but her gaze stopped on Nebby and Storm. "I—I know you. You're a part of the Wi—" She caught herself and looked at Rupert.

"It's okay, Mom. I know they're part of the Witches Council. And I know they forced you to work for them."

"I'm the Nebulous Witch." Nebby held out her hand, and his mother tentatively shook it. "Ah, now that we're face-to-face, I do think I recognize you, but we've never actually met."

After a moment's hesitation, Rupert's mother began to speak. "I've only ever talked to the Fairfoul Witch and the Midnight Witch," she said, her voice sounding a little timid. "They forbid me from speaking to anyone. And I've only stepped foot in the lair during off-hours."

"That explains it, then," Nebby said warmly. "I'm sorry for anything you went through because of them. We aren't all quite so difficult, are we Storm?"

Storm walked over and pinched his mom's cheeks. "Hello, I'm Storm. Lovely, *lovely* to meet you!"

"Rupert?" his mom said, calling for help.

Rupert pried Storm off his mother's face. And then he told his mother everything, starting at the very beginning. He told her all about Mrs. Frabbleknacker's trip to the dump, all about her horrible lessons, all about the help he had been giving Sandy, all about Mrs. Frabbleknacker's true identity as the Fairfoul Witch, and about the great rabbit fiasco.

"Back up!" his mother interrupted. "Your teacher was the *Fairfoul Witch*?"

Sandy nodded vigorously, and Storm shrugged.

"But—but *why*?"

Nebby gently rested her hand on his mother's shoulder. "After listening to the Fairfoul Witch's testimony, the Council realizes now that we severely underestimated how much she loved to practice her punishments. Last summer, she saw that a post for a fifth-grade teacher was available, and she took the job. Because, truly, where better to practice cruel magic than with a class of kids? After all, who would believe them?"

Rupert glared at his mother, and she guiltily slouched.

Nebby kept talking. "Can you believe she had been lying to her own Witches Council? She sneaked out in the morning when we all thought she was sleeping, and none of us ever wanted to disturb her sleep because she is a renowned grouch when she wakes up. I can't believe she pulled the wool over my eyes for so long."

"Don't blame yourself, Nebby," Sandy said brightly. "She fooled us all. You know, Rupert always smelled very funny when he came home from school. I should have recognized her scent way earlier."

Rupert's mother put a hand on his shoulder. "You tried to tell me all about Mrs. Frabbleknacker, and I wouldn't listen."

"That's okay, Mom," Rupert said. "Allison's parents didn't believe her either, and she came home with mustache and beard. And Manny's parents didn't even notice he was gone!"

"Gone?"

Rupert nodded. "Mrs. Frabbleknacker turned him into our class pet."

His mother steadied herself by gripping the basement table.

Nebby pursed her lips. "We have reason to believe that the Fairfoul Witch was using potions on local parents to make them forget about their children."

"Well, that's horrible!" said Rupert's mother. "That witch is the most horrible witch I've ever had the misfortune to meet."

Rupert shuffled his feet. Then he took a deep breath and asked the question that had been gnawing at him for a while. "Mom, why did you steal that forbidden potion? You must have known you'd be punished."

"Yes, that was certainly a risk."

"Why did you do it, then?"

She pulled him into a tight hug. "Because I wanted you in my life, Rupert. You're more important to me than anything else in the world."

Rupert swallowed a choked-up feeling in his throat, and he buried his face into her middle.

His mother brushed his hair with her hand. "When I look at you, I know I made the right choice. You're worth it, Rupert. You are so worth every bit of my debt, and I'll be glad to pay it off for as long as I live."

"You won't have to," Rupert said, and he pulled the signed contract from his pocket. "The Witches Council promised to leave us alone."

His mother tore the contract from him, her eyes widening as she read. "How did you—"

"It was Sandy," Rupert said. "And Nebby and Storm, too—they helped."

His mother read over the contract again and wiped the silent tears off her cheeks. When she finally spoke again, her voice was choked, but she cracked a smile wider than Rupert had seen on her in years.

"You were right, Rupert," his mother said. "You were right all along."

"About the witches?"

"No, about Sandy. She's a good friend."

"The best," Rupert agreed.

Sandy smiled and blushed a shade so red she almost looked purple.

The Bar Exam

W HEN R UPERT WALKED INTO SCHOOL ON F RI-day, the whole class sat silently. News that Mrs. Frabbleknacker decided to step down from her post before the school year was over spread across the town like an outbreak of lice. Only Rupert knew the truth—that Mrs. Frabbleknacker, at the behest of the Witches Council, had decided to permanently retire from teaching.

Rupert took his seat next to Kyle and Allison. "Good morning," he said to no one in particular. "How's it going?"

"Shhhh!" Allison hissed.

"Are you crazy?" Kyle said.

"Don't talk until we see who our teacher is,"

Hal said. "What if she's worse than Mrs. Frabbleknacker?"

Rupert smiled. "She won't be," he said.

At that moment, a man burst into the room and wrote his name underneath the spot in the chalkboard where Mrs. Frabbleknacker had carved LIFE IS FAIR, AND FAIR IS FOUL.

"Good morning, class," he said.

Nobody spoke. Everyone stared at him with big doe eyes.

"Oh, well," the man said, rubbing his hands in his hair. "I'm Mr. Splinkle. I, erm . . . wrote my name on the board here as you can see. Feel free to copy it down."

Everyone scribbled his name as fast as possible.

"Er, well, today we're going to work on science."

Everybody cringed.

"Hmmm?" Mr. Splinkle said. "Well, I thought we'd talk about different ecosystems. Can anybody name one?"

Poor, brave Bruno raised his hand. "The ocean?" he said.

"Almost," Mr. Splinkle said. The class cowered,

waiting for him to institute a punishment on poor, brave Bruno. But instead, Mr. Splinkle continued. "You're right in concept, but technically it's called the Marine Ecosystem."

The whole class exhaled. No punishment, not even for getting a question wrong.

Mr. Splinkle taught the most boring lesson that Rupert had ever endured. Then he taught an even more boring grammar lesson about gerunds. Then he taught, if possible, an even more boring-beyond-boring math lesson about multiplying fractions.

It was the most wonderful school day Rupert had had in a very long time.

After class, he waited outside the door for Kaleigh, Allison, Kyle, Manny, Hal, Bruno, and the rest of his classmates, but Mr. Splinkle came out first.

"Good day today, eh, Rupert?" he said.

"Yes, sir!"

"I think I'm going to like your class. Though you're all as quiet as rabbits." He walked to the teachers' lounge, humming to himself.

His classmates started filing out of the classroom, and they all huddled together.

"What do you think?" Bruno asked.

"I like him," said Hal. "I think he's the best teacher ever."

"I'm going to bring him an apple," said Kaleigh.

"I'm going to bring him two," Allison said.

"Let's meet up tomorrow before class," Manny suggested.

They decided to arrive ten minutes early tomorrow—and some of them were even going to the playground to hang around after school today, but Rupert had somewhere very special and very important to be.

He ran down the hallway and pushed his way through the double doors. Outside, his mother waited for him with a cake that read *Congratulations, Sand Witch!*

"Microwavable cake?" Rupert asked.

"Not this time," his mother said. "This one's home-made." She paused for a moment. "Rupert, I know I didn't believe you about Mrs. Frabbleknacker, and I feel horrible about it."

"Don't," he said.

"But I do. I really do. And I will believe you from now on, no matter what," his mother said.

Rupert grinned. "Okay. Let's test this new mother," he said. He cleared his throat. "I am a flying elephant from Butterly—"

"—I'll believe you from now on, in *moderation*," his mother said, ruffling his hair.

They walked along in silence for a moment, and Rupert thought about how things with his mother had changed. In the days that followed, Rupert and his mother cooked dinner together, drank hot chocolate, "funky little boogie danced" on the countertop, and even re-plotted their overgrown garden together.

Three days is a long time, thought Rupert. It was enough to repair his relationship with his mother, but it was also enough time to lose contact with Sandy. Rupert hadn't seen her since they had stopped the rabbits in town. Whenever he called, Nebby refused to hand off the phone because Sandy was cramming for her Bar Exam. Which, according to Nebby, was going to be extra-grueling for her because the Witches Council was still angry about the Great Rabbit Fiasco.

He was disappointed that he couldn't talk to her or coach her in the last few days, but he understood that she really had to buckle down and focus. That was why he asked his mom to take him to Sandy's testing facility—the high school gymnasium—after school.

He cocked his head to check his mother's watch.

"Mom, we're going to miss her!"

"We'll be fine," she told him.

Rupert ran forward. He hoped the Bar Exam wasn't already over. It had started a half hour before he was finished school.

"Don't run ahead," she said. "I'm still going at the same pace, and I won't get any faster if you do."

"Come *on*, Mom!" he said.

"Are you carrying a cake, Rupert?"

Finally, he and his mother rounded the street corner near the high school, and they walked over to where a cluster of witches was standing with balloons and kazoos, waiting for their respective witchlings to finish their exams. Nebby had a party hat on, and Rupert thought it looked rather silly. He was going to say something about it until he saw the worried look on her face.

"Don't worry," Rupert said, giving Nebby a quick hug.

She smiled softly at him.

An unfamiliar witch marched over to his mother. "Lovely cake," the witch said, swiping a bit of frosting with her finger. "Mmmm, delicious!"

"The Hibbly Witch," Nebby introduced before turning to look anxiously at the gymnasium doors.

Just then, the doors swung open and a knotty-haired, pointy-faced, squinty-eyed witchling strutted out. It was Witchling Four. "I'm a full-fledged witch, now," she bragged to her guardian, the Cold-wind Witch. "I'm the Floodburst Witch."

Rupert ran up to her. "Did Witchling Two go yet?"

"She was right after me, which means she's probably in the middle of flopping right about now," the Floodburst Witch said, sticking her tongue out at Rupert and brushing past him.

They walked away together, and Nebby bit her lip. "I hope she passes."

"She will," said Rupert.

"She better," said Nebby, tugging on the strings of her party hat. "I only wear party hats on very special days."

They fell into silence, and Rupert stared at the

gymnasium, longing to watch. And then he got an idea.

"I have to use the bathroom—be right back!" Rupert said, and he dashed toward the side door of the high school.

"But you might miss her!" Rupert's mom shouted after him.

But he kept running. He dashed down the hallways, following signs for the gymnasium. He stopped just before the double doors. *Rats, no windows.*

Out of the corner of his eye, he saw an air-conditioning vent, and he grinned. He popped the cover off and climbed on through. He crawled up eagerly and stopped in front of another air-conditioning grate—one that faced inside the gym.

Sandy was sweating over a cauldron, but Rupert had no idea what she could be brewing. She wiped her forehead with her sleeve and kept popping ingredients in the mix. Simmer. Stir. Swipe with her finger and taste a nibble. She smiled confidently every step of the way.

Rupert looked at the table across from her and saw a collection of witches. There was the Fairfoul Witch, of course. And he recognized the Midnight

Witch, the Lightning Witch, the Thunder Witch, and Storm. Rupert had never seen the other two witches before, and he assumed they were visiting witches from Harkshire or Foxbury, which made Rupert feel better. They were bound to have a more objective opinion of Sandy's abilities.

After brewing her potion for a while, she finally lifted the ladle to her mouth and cried, "Done!"

The haggard-looking Lightning Witch hobbled up to Sandy, poured a bit of the potion into a goblet, and drank from it.

The Lightning Witch smacked her lips. "Tastes exactly like egg salad. Well done."

Rupert choked back a laugh. She made an *egg salad* potion for her exam?

He leaned forward a bit, trying to catch the Fairfoul Witch's reaction, but he couldn't see anything until she stood up and leered over the table.

"You've passed your WHATs. You've passed your potions." The Fairfoul Witch scowled. "But can you pass your spell portion of the exam?"

Sandy nodded. Then her eyes traveled upward and to the left—she stared at the air-conditioning vent and nodded.

Rupert's stomach leaped—Sandy knew he was there!

She turned back to the board of examiners. "Give me *any* spell. I know I can do it!"

"We'll give you a series of things to conjure up," said the Midnight Witch. "Ready?"

Sandy nodded.

"Shoe."

"Blue," Sandy said with a snap of her fingers. A shoe appeared in her hands.

"Shirt."

"Dirt," Sandy said. A shirt appeared on the ground.

"Jetpack."

Sandy laughed. "Oh, that's easy. Pet sack!" she said, snapping her fingers. As expected, a Jetpack appeared.

"Vat is *zis?*" The Thunder Witch said. "Vhy is it zat vat you are saying is deeferent zan vat you are conjuring?"

"It's my little trick," Sandy said. "That's how I conjure. It's foolproof."

"*Is* it now?" the Fairfoul Witch smirked. "Then how about you conjure me a penguin?"

Rupert gripped the bars of the air-conditioning vent with white knuckles as he realized *there was no rhyme for penguin.*

"P-penguin?" Sandy said in a small voice.

"Sure," the Fairfoul Witch said. "Or, forget the penguin. Conjure me an olive."

"An olive," Sandy said, deadpan.

"No, no, you're right. An olive isn't *interesting* enough. Instead, you can put a chimney on this roof. No—rather, conjure me something purple."

None of these words rhymed with anything. The Fairfoul Witch was prepared to stump her, and now Sandy would fail her exam, have her powers stripped, and be forced to leave Gliverstoll forever. Rupert hid his face in his hands. He didn't want to watch this . . . this bloodbath.

Sandy stood there with her hands limp, looking like she didn't know what to do.

The Fairfoul Witch threw her head back and cackled. The Midnight Witch joined in, but the other witches seated at the table looked rather uncomfortable.

"You already had a name picked out, didn't you, Witchling Two? What was it that the loathsome little Campbell boy called you? *The Sand Witch*? A little premature to pick out a name before you even pass your exam, don't you think?" The Fairfoul Witch leaned close to Sandy. "You want to earn the title? Conjure me a sandwich, then. Something delicious."

Rupert quickly went through the alphabet and realized that there was no rhyme for sandwich, either. His thoughts buzzed about—he needed to step in and save her, but how?

Sandy closed her eyes and took a deep breath. When she opened her eyes again, she looked firmly into the Fairfoul Witch's piercing eyes.

"Well?" Sandy said carefully. "Which is it? Which of these things would you like me to conjure?"

This, apparently, wasn't the reaction the Fairfoul Witch was expecting.

"You won't pass unless you conjure them all," she snapped.

"Okay!" Sandy said brightly. "Engine, knowledge, kidney, burble, and a grand old perky canned-snitch!" She snapped her fingers.

Rupert pressed his face against the grate.

A penguin popped up next to Sandy. Then she uncurled her left hand to reveal a tiny olive. The ceiling rumbled and a chimney popped up. In her right hand, she revealed a purple locket.

Everyone except the Fairfoul Witch clapped.

"Where's the sandwich?" she hissed. "You can't pass without that!"

"Check your bag," Sandy said coolly. "I think you'll find a bland, cold turkey sandwich."

The Fairfoul Witch dug in her bag and pulled out a turkey hoagie wrapped in paper.

Sandy bowed, and the table clapped for her. Storm smiled extra wide.

But the Fairfoul Witch scowled, baring her inordinately pointy teeth. She picked up the table and threw it across the room, where it narrowly missed the waddling penguin. Then, with a flourish of her cloak, the Fairfoul Witch stormed out of the gymnasium. The Midnight Witch copied the Fairfoul Witch in every gesture and marched out behind her.

There was a tittering from the rest of the board, and one of the witches Rupert didn't recognize stood up. "Well, I'll be!" she said. "We *never* act in such an unsightly manner in Foxbury. This witchling obviously has the skill and ingenuity it takes to be a full-fledged witch."

"Vitchling Two, ve're proud to present you with ze title of Vitch," said the Thunder Witch.

"From here on out, you will now be known as the Sand Witch," the Lightning Witch said with a smile.

With tears in her eyes, Storm popped up from her seat and engulfed Sandy in a great big hug.

"Can't—breathe—Storm—"

Storm let go.

Sandy thanked the witches and ran out of the gymnasium. Rupert quickly turned around and began wiggling his way out of the vent, but then suddenly it seemed that the vent was much wider than it was before. So wide, in fact, that Rupert didn't even have to crawl. He stood up and walked. When he reached the grate by the gymnasium entrance, he found that the grate was the size of a large door, and so he swung it open and jumped out.

Sandy stood there, waiting for him, excitedly bouncing.

"I suppose the growing vent was your doing, Sand Witch?" Rupert said.

She giggled, and Rupert ran and hugged her.

"I PASSED!"

"I know! But how did you conjure up all those things that didn't have rhymes?"

Sandy grinned. "Nebby had a feeling that the Fairfoul Witch would try to stump me like that. So she made a list of hyrax words that don't rhyme with anything exactly, and Storm helped me practice how to conjure them."

"But how could you?"

"We practiced zebra-rhymes," she said.

"Zebra-rhymes?"

"What's that you humans call them? Half-rhymes? Near-rhymes? Quarter-rhymes? Almost rhymes? Partial rhymes?"

"And that works?"

She nodded. "Even when my spells on you went horribly horribly wrong, a lot of times it just *sounded* like something, but it didn't have to be perfect. If it sounds enough like something else, there's a whole lot of ways my spellwork could go wrong," she said proudly.

"Not anymore," Rupert said, "because you're a real witch now!"

"Let's go tell everyone!" she squealed. She grabbed

his hand and ran with him through the high school—
and then out the doors to where his mother, Nebby,
and the remaining witch guardians stood.

"WELL?" everyone said.

Sandy did a cartwheel. "I PASSED!" she said.

Nebby threw the Sand Witch up into the air and
paraded her around town on her shoulders. Rupert
followed, clapping and hooting and hollering. And
Rupert's mother walked behind them, making sure
to hold the cake steady.

Later, Rupert and his mother ended up at Nebby's
clean and pristine lair for celebratory cake, tea, and
scones.

"More sugar?" Nebby asked Rupert's mother.

Rupert's mother picked up a sugar cube with the
tongs and dropped it into the tea. "You must have
done wonderfully," Rupert's mother said.

"I did, I did!" Sandy said with a grin. "You should
have seen me, Nebby! Zebra rhyme here, zebra
rhyme there! It was vernacular!"

"Spectacular," everyone corrected, and then they
all laughed.

Rupert smiled. He never thought—not in a million years—that he could help a witch with her

magic. He never thought that his best friend would be a witch. He never thought that he would prove that his horrible rotten teacher was a witch. He never thought his mother would actually believe him about his horrible rotten teacher. And he especially never thought that he would peaceably have tea with his witch-hating mother and three witches.

"Psst!" Sandy whispered under the sound of the adults talking.

"What?"

"Come with me!"

Rupert and Sandy excused themselves from the table and ran upstairs to Sandy's room. It looked just like her lair at Pexale Close—all cluttered and musty and cramped. It was the only room in Nebby's perfect house that was an absolute mess.

Rupert watched as stacks of papers blew around in the breeze that was coming from Sandy's open window. Rupert walked over to the window and looked out—she had the most wonderful seaside view, with the orange sun setting beneath a purple sky.

"Hey, look," Rupert said. "It's your favorite color."

Sandy squealed.

"Sandy? Thanks for everything. Really."

"No, thank *you*, Rupert! You are the best apprentice ever . . ." Sandy smiled, her ears turning bright pink. She turned back toward the closet and dug through piles of clothes. At last, she seemed to find what she was looking for because she turned around with her hands behind her back.

"And now I'm going to give you a little treat. I hope you like heights," she said, and she whipped a broom out from behind her back.

If anyone were patrolling the skies for the witches that night, he would have seen one broom holding a young girl in a floral dress squealing with joy and a boy cackling like a witch. It must have been a very confusing sight, indeed.

 The End

Acknowledgments

Nancy Conescu, who welcomed Rupert and Sandy into the greatest possible home with open arms; who always took care of them lovingly; who understood their story better than anyone (probably including me); whose clever insights made my jokes sharper and helped me grow as a storyteller; whose astute influence is imprinted on every page.

Stacey Friedberg, who is a certified title genius, who always answers my never-ending questions with warmth, and whose brilliant editorial notes always made me excited to dive back in.

The Penguin Team, whose endless support and tireless behind-the-scenes work make me so thankful and appreciative.

Friends, family, coworkers, and teachers, who have supported, inspired, and encouraged me during this adventure.

Michele Rubin, who held my hand through the first half of this journey, and whose enthusiasm and engulfing hugs brightened all of my days.

Brianne Johnson, who loved Rupert and Sandy first, who made my dreams come true, and who believed in me long before she ever had a manuscript in her hands. To you, I owe everything.

I love you all more than all the grape lollipops in the world . . . and that's a whole lot!